If Derrick did
ing at a girl. A slen
legs that—

Catherine Markham   pushed away from the railing. Catherine was quiet, well-bred, and demure—he didn't think he'd heard her say more than ten words the entire time he'd known her. But surely not . . . Catherine Markham wasn't the kind of brazen female to stride about the docks wearing boy's clothing. Surely the lad before him was just a boy and nothing more.

As if in answer to his unspoken question, the "boy" turned toward the dog and a strand of hair escaped the hat. The long tendril curled over one shoulder, glinting gold in the morning light.

Derrick cursed out loud. What in the world was that blasted girl doing?

DON'T MISS A SINGLE
AVON TRUE ROMANCE

SAMANTHA AND THE COWBOY
by Lorraine Heath

BELLE AND THE BEAU
by Beverly Jenkins

ANNA AND THE DUKE
by Kathryn Smith

GWYNETH AND THE THIEF
by Margaret Moore

NICOLA AND THE VISCOUNT
by Meg Cabot

CATHERINE AND THE PIRATE
by Karen Hawkins

MIRANDA AND THE WARRIOR
by Elaine Barbieri

AN AVON TRUE ROMANCE

Catherine
and the
Pirate

KAREN HAWKINS

AVON BOOKS
An Imprint of HarperCollinsPublishers

FIND TRUE LOVE!
www.avontrueromance.com

An Avon True Romance is a trademark of HarperCollins Publishers Inc.

Catherine and the Pirate
Copyright © 2002 by Karen Hawkins

Printed in the United States of America.
For information address HarperCollins Children's Books,
a division of HarperCollins Publishers, 1350 Avenue of the Americas,
New York, NY 10019.

Library of Congress Catalog Card Number: 2002090317
ISBN 0-06-447346-5

First Avon edition, 2002

AVON TRADEMARK REG. U.S. PAT. OFF. AND IN OTHER COUNTRIES,
MARCA REGISTRADA, HECHO EN U.S.A.

❖

Visit us on the World Wide Web!
www.harperteen.com

To Kim Hawkins and Jennifer Brumit,

who had the great idea to write a pirate book.

Thank you for your inspiration!

Catherine
and the
Pirate

❧

CHAPTER ONE

High Hall, Massachusetts
1777

Catherine Markham gripped the stiff scrap of paper. "I knew it," she whispered, her fingers trembling. "Royce is alive."

Happiness flooded through her and she slid to the floor beside the desk, a single tear slipping down her cheek. Since the day a few weeks earlier when Uncle Elliot had told Catherine that her brother had drowned, his heavily loaded frigate sunk off the rocky Carolina coast after a ruthless attack by the British, her life had become a painful blur.

Why did Royce have to go on that blasted trip? Catherine asked herself for the hundredth time. He usually stayed home, but he'd been anxious to show support for the Continental Army as they struggled to throw off British oppression, and he'd decided to see to the shipment of leather and iron himself. The shipment was destined for New York, where a convoy of carts would convey it to General Washington's army.

Catherine sighed. Royce had always been drawn to the sea. Four years ago, he had been the captain of one of Father's most profitable ships. Only thirteen at the time, Catherine had idolized her brother, who was a full twelve years older than she, waiting excitedly for him to return from his voyages. He always brought her something—silk from China, an engraved ivory tusk from India, a silver chain from England. And she, in return, wrote him long, long letters of life at High Hill Manor.

After Catherine's parents were killed in a carriage accident four years ago, Royce had come home, and together he and Catherine had struggled to heal what was left of their family. It had taken a number of sad months, but eventually life had fallen back into a comfortable pattern. Catherine had come to discover that, all in all, it was an ideal arrangement. Royce trusted Catherine's judgment and listened to her thoughts and suggestions, and in return, she respected his opinions and listened to his advice. In a way, he was not only her brother but also her best friend.

And she had not been able to believe he was gone forever.

She blinked away tears as she read the note once again. Torn and dirty, the ink had smeared in places and the spelling was far from perfect. But the message was clear: The author claimed to have rescued Royce from the sea and to have him in his care. But it was the last sentence that sent chills through Catherine—if the Markhams wanted to see Royce again, they would have to bring fifty gold pieces to the Red Rooster Inn in Savannah by the first of June.

"The first of June," Catherine whispered. "That's in less than two weeks."

Her heart thudded hard against her chest. Surely Uncle Elliot had already paid the ransom. Catherine's uncle had come to stay at High Hall as soon as he'd heard the news of the attack on Royce's ship. Catherine wasn't overly fond of her uncle; he seemed very cold and unemotional to her.

Still, as much as Catherine disliked Uncle Elliot's overbearing presence, she had to admit that he had been helpful since Royce's disappearance, taking over the daily duties of running the Markham shipping business and fending off the many people who came to call and offer their condolences.

For Catherine, that had hurt the worst—how quickly people believed that Royce would never return. Every visitor who arrived at High Hall in the days after Royce's ship sank seemed to add more credence to the one thing Catherine would not believe: that her brother was dead. And now . . . her fingers tightened on the note and a small smile began to curve her lips. She'd been right; her brother was alive.

She wondered why Uncle Elliot hadn't told her about

the note. She knew he wouldn't leave Royce helpless in the clutches of a group of madmen. Perhaps her uncle had already paid the ransom and Royce was even now on his way home and it was going to be a huge and wonderful surprise when—

"Catherine?" Uncle Elliot stood in the open doorway, the light from the hallway outlining his broad shoulders. He was built like all the Markham men—tall, strong, and muscular. "What are you doing in here?"

She got to her feet, feeling somehow guilty even though she had every right to be there, at Royce's desk. "I came to get some paper to write a thank-you note to the governor for the kind letter he sent. I—I found this on the desk." She held out the note.

Uncle Elliot strode forward and took the note, his brows lowering in a quick frown. The late afternoon light briefly touched the lines on his face and Catherine noted that he looked more and more like Father as the years passed. The main difference between the two men was that while Father had always laughed and had a tendency to see the good in everything around him, Uncle Elliot was more somber, less playful. He rarely smiled, and even then it was more a polite gesture than anything else.

"I'm sorry, Catherine." Uncle Elliot turned away briefly, placing the note back on the desk. "I should have told you about this, but I didn't want you to worry and—"

"You paid the ransom." Catherine took a step closer,

smoothing her dress in a nervous gesture. "Royce is coming home soon, isn't he? Did you send a ship for him? Or will he—"

"No." Uncle Elliot faced her now, his expression troubled.

Her heart thudded harder. "What do you mean?"

"The letter came only two days after the attack. It is obviously a sad attempt by a very desperate group of persons to profit from our grief." Uncle Elliot shook his head gravely. "I can't allow that."

"You . . . you believe the note is a fake?" That thought hadn't occurred to her; she'd been too relieved to think that Royce might be alive. She looked back at the note. What if it wasn't fake? What if Royce was still alive somewhere, wounded and waiting for them to rescue him? A sense of urgency pushed her forward. "Uncle Elliot, if there's even a chance that Royce might be alive, then we must do what we can."

"It would be a waste of time. There were witnesses who saw your brother go into the water. Several stated that not only did they see him go into the water, but that he was unconscious after the mast fell across him. He cannot be alive."

The images Uncle Elliot painted were painful, and Catherine had to force them away. "They never found his body."

"It was nighttime. They wouldn't have been able to see

it, especially with the amount of debris left behind after the British attack." He took a step forward and gathered her hands in his, his fingers strangely cold. "Catherine, listen to me. I know these last few weeks have been difficult, but you must accept that Royce is lost to us. We have to go on from here."

Catherine shook her head, tears gathering, her throat tightening. Royce had to be alive—he had to be. She pulled her hands free from her uncle's grasp. "W-we will pay the ransom, Uncle Elliot. Perhaps it isn't fake. Perhaps it's real and—"

"Royce is gone. There's nothing we can do about it, and the sooner you accept that fact, the easier it will be for you."

"How can you say such a thing? We are talking about Royce, your own nephew—"

"I know who he is!" Uncle Elliot said abruptly, his mouth pressed in a straight line. "I care about him, too. But you must listen to reason. Even if Royce did manage to survive the attack, even if he was abducted by these . . . Whoever they are, they aren't men of honor. I know the type, and they'd as soon lie as breathe."

"How do you know these men are lying? What if they really do have Royce in their clutches?"

"If Royce was alive when his captors wrote this letter, then why isn't it written in his hand? Why didn't they offer some proof that he was alive?"

She swallowed. "Perhaps he was ill, or injured."

Uncle Elliot raked a hand through his hair, suddenly looking older than his fifty-six years. "Catherine, listen to yourself. You aren't making sense. These ruffians didn't offer any proof because there was none to be had. I have thought and thought of this until I can think no more. As painful as it is, we must accept that Royce is lost to us. It will be easier for you."

"I can't!" The words came from her heart and they echoed loudly in the room.

Uncle Elliot sighed heavily. "Then believe what you will; it will not change the facts. Meanwhile we have other things to discuss." He walked behind the desk and sat down in the large leather chair that Royce had brought back from his travels to Spain. "The solicitor is coming tomorrow to read your brother's will. You and I must be present, as we are the only two beneficiaries. I hope you won't—"

Catherine backed away. "I won't go to a reading of the will. Not until we know for certain that Royce is dead."

Uncle Elliot's jaw tightened. "We must settle things. Your brother would expect you to do no less. If we do not act quickly, the shipping business that your father and Royce worked so hard to build could fail." He hesitated, and then said in a gentler voice, "These are uncertain times, Catherine. The war with Britain has interfered with the company's operation—we've had three ships sunk in as many months. Things are precarious at best and we must protect the family's interests at all costs."

Catherine's jaw tightened. "You seem to care more about Markham Tea Company than my brother!"

A dull red color touched Uncle Elliot's cheeks. "That's not true. I admit that I was somewhat . . . chagrined when I discovered that your father had left the entire bulk of the company to Royce. But I have since come to realize that it was for the best. Your brother was a remarkable business-man. He doubled the company's worth in a very short time, hired better captains, and developed new contacts in foreign countries. Your father would have been proud.

"Meanwhile I . . ." Uncle Elliot looked down at the neat stack of correspondence that lay on the desk. "I thought that your father would have recognized the work I'd put into the company. But he didn't see fit to do so, and that is that."

Catherine heard the pain in Uncle Elliot's voice and it surprised her. "Uncle Elliot, Father would never have hurt your feelings intentionally. He was very fond of you."

Uncle Elliot managed a faint smile. "Of course. I'm certain he had reasons for doing what he did. However, what has happened is over now." He looked at Catherine, his thick brows lowered over the bridge of his nose. After a long moment, his face softened slightly and he reached over and gave her hand a quick squeeze. "You are a dear child. And when you inherit the company from Royce, you will need all the help I am able to give you."

Inherit the company? Catherine shook her head. "I don't want it. I wouldn't know what to—"

"Don't worry. I will be here to assist you as much as I can. But—"

"It's not appropriate to discuss that now," Catherine said quickly.

Not now. Not ever.

Elliot nodded as if he understood. "Of course. It's too soon, isn't it? I should never have brought up the subject. Now, if you will excuse me, my dear, I have things to see to before dinner this evening. In the meantime, why don't you retire for a few hours and rest?"

Catherine's hands tightened into fists. Now that she'd seen the note, resting was the last thing she wanted to do. She frowned at Uncle Elliot. How could he be so calm when there was a possibility that Royce was alive somewhere and injured, perhaps fatally?

She started to say as much, when her gaze fell on the note. Instead of arguing, she cleared her throat and said, "I believe you're right, Uncle Elliot. Perhaps I should rest in my room."

He nodded. "Very good, my dear. I shall see you at dinner."

Catherine slowly walked out of the room, her mind racing. Uncle Elliot had made up his mind about the ransom note, but she hadn't. She climbed the wide staircase and made her way to her bedchamber and once there, sank onto a seat by the window.

Her bedchamber was decorated with beautiful mahogany furniture, including a four-poster bed along one wall, its blue velvet hangings echoed in the expensive Aubusson rug. The blue lace curtains that hung over the windows framed a breathtaking view of the garden and the fields beyond.

Catherine took great pride in seeing that the garden looked wonderful every year, filled with her mother's favorite flowers. Almost every evening she'd open the windows and let the cool spring breeze bring the scent of the flowers into her room, but today she didn't have the heart. Instead of opening the window, she leaned against it and stared at the colorful garden without seeing it.

As much as she hated to admit it, Uncle Elliot's reasoning was sound—there were those who did indeed attempt to capture ships in order to detain wealthy travelers and attempt to get money from their innocent families. Certainly Uncle Elliot was right when he said that most of the time the abducted person was never returned—at least, not alive.

Still, Catherine was certain she'd heard of several cases where the missing person was actually returned. And it was that faint memory, along with the inexplicable feeling that somehow Royce was alive and well, that led her to believe that Uncle Elliot was mistaken.

"But we have only two weeks," she murmured, resting her forehead against the cool glass. It would take at least a month to change Uncle Elliot's mind. He was as stubborn as Father had been.

She sighed, silently weighing her options. If Uncle Elliot didn't help her, then she was on her own. *She* would have to find the money and deliver it to Savannah. She slowly straightened. That was exactly what she had to do: rescue Royce herself. He would have done the same for her. She knew that.

Her chest tightened as she began to think about what such a daring enterprise would entail. First she would have to find a way to Savannah. As she was thinking of the possible ways to do this, a side door in the garden opened and Uncle Elliot emerged, dressed in riding clothes. Every afternoon at exactly two, he rode down to the docks to see the latest arrival for the Markham Tea Company.

Catherine hurried to close the curtains of her bedchamber. Now was the time. It would be hours before he returned and, since he'd suggested that she rest, he'd not expect to see her until dinner. But where would she go? How would she get to Savannah in such a short time?

Her gaze fell on a tiny replica of a ship that Royce had given her only a few months before. "That's it," she murmured. She'd go to the harbor and find a ship to carry her to Savannah. It would take her weeks to travel by horse. But by sea, the trip could be completed within a week.

Perhaps Derrick St. John's ship would be in harbor. When their father's death had forced Royce to take responsibility for the company from behind a desk instead of upon the seas as he'd loved, he'd hired his best friend, Derrick, as lead captain. After a time, Derrick had managed to buy the ship outright from Royce, and now he owned the ship he captained, though he still ran shipments for his old friend.

The thought of Derrick made Catherine hesitate. The tall, dark-haired man was not someone she normally would ask for assistance. Though he was close to Royce, he tended to be less polite to Catherine. She rather suspected that she thought her childish and a nuisance, a fact that irritated her to no end. Whenever Derrick was about, Catherine made it a point not to speak directly to him, a very poor effort on her part to show the handsome young man that she didn't care what he thought about her. Still, he wouldn't refuse to help, not with Royce's life at stake. If there was one thing Catherine knew, it was that Derrick would do anything to help his friend.

Many people wondered at Royce's friendship with Derrick—the young man had been a known hellion, defying his family to the point of taking up with a set of ruffians that had dabbled in everything from thievery to out-and-out piracy.

Catherine didn't know the exact details of the handsome sea captain's transgressions, but she knew her brother trusted the man with his most important cargos. And that, she decided, was all she needed to know. Royce did not place his confidence in many people.

Royce's trust in Derrick had paid off—the younger man had a way with a ship that few did, and he managed to turn a profit on every voyage.

With the British on the prowl, threatening to blow every American ship they saw out of the water, Catherine knew she'd need someone with a fast ship who knew the safest route to Savannah. And Derrick St. John was that person. A fresh wave of hope lifted her heart.

She jumped up, went to her wardrobe, and began to dig through her clothing. In the depths of the bottom drawer she found a loose white shirt, a pair of Royce's old breeches, and some worn leather boots. She'd used these when she and Royce would occasionally go riding about the woods surrounding High Hall.

Catherine hadn't worn the clothes in a year, and the last time she wore them, they'd hung so loosely that Royce had called her "Rag Man" for weeks. Now they fit all too well. "I'll need a coat or something to go over this," Catherine muttered, looking down at where her chest pushed the soft fabric out. Maybe she could borrow the stable boy's shapeless brown coat.

Now if only Derrick was in port . . . Catherine didn't have any way of knowing. The British were running their ships up and down the coast and attacking any ship that might be carrying goods or supplies to the Americans, which meant there was no set schedule of arrivals in Boston Harbor.

Catherine tossed her hat on the bed and then tied back her hair, wishing she had something other than a blue ribbon. It was too long to secure in a bun, but perhaps . . . she opened the door to her closet and rummaged through the boxes that sat in one corner. Finally, she found what she was looking for: a large brown hat she used when picking berries for cook to make pies.

She tucked her hair beneath the hat, then looked at herself in the mirror. If she borrowed the brown coat and stayed in the shadows, she might pass for a boy. Sighing, she turned from the mirror. It would have to do. Catherine collected the pillowcase, opened the door to her room, and peered out into the empty hallway. If anyone saw her and reported it to Uncle Elliot, he would try to stop her, protesting that it wasn't safe for her to travel alone, especially not in the middle of a war.

But Catherine didn't care. This was an emergency and she had to reach Royce as soon as possible.

She waited a few moments, until she was certain none of the servants was nearby. Then she left her room and quickly made her way back to the library, her booted feet quietly thumping on the wood floor.

Once she reached the library, she took a deep breath and then glanced inside the open doorway. She gave a sigh of relief when she saw that the room was empty. She quickly entered, leaving the door the way it had been, slightly open so she could see the hallway. She crossed to the desk, then opened the bottom drawer. Catherine emptied the drawer, setting the stack of papers and books to one side. Then she gently pulled the empty drawer completely out of the desk and turned it over.

One corner hit the wooden floor and thunked loudly, the sound echoing like a gunshot. Catherine held her breath and waited, her eyes on the door, but no one stormed into the room. After a long moment, she released her breath and moved to one side so that the slit of light from between the drawn curtains fell on the drawer.

With trembling hands she felt around the wooden trim until she found what she was looking for. The tiny notch felt more like a flaw in the wood, but Catherine knew otherwise. She fumbled with the indentation and the bottom of the drawer fell away to reveal a secret compartment.

"Thank you, Royce," Catherine breathed. He'd shown her the small cubbyhole not long ago. Money for emergencies, he'd told her. Catherine knew he was worried the English would invade Boston and that they would have to flee, leaving everything behind, but this was just as dire an emergency, if not more.

Catherine lifted the bag of coins and tucked it into her pocket, then scooted behind the desk to replace the drawer. She had just lifted it into place when a faint creak sounded. Catherine froze.

The door to the study had needed oil for years. Royce had said he'd see to it, yet somehow he'd never found the time. Her heart pounding in her ears, Catherine closed her eyes and prayed. It was all she could do. If any of the servants found her here, there would be questions.

No other sound came. Catherine waited, her back stiff, her knees aching from the cold, hard floor. After a few moments, she could stand it no more and she leaned forward to peep around the corner of the desk.

A woolly face peered back. "George!" Catherine whispered, relief making her grin. She grabbed her dog by the head and hugged him fiercely. "What are you doing in the house?"

Father had given George to her four years ago, on Catherine's thirteenth birthday, a mere two weeks before he and Mother were killed in the carriage accident. It had made Catherine love the mutt even more despite the fact that it soon became apparent that George was by no means as well behaved as Royce's dogs. His spaniels came when called, sat when ordered, and could complete a whole list of tricks at a command, while George never seemed to follow any command.

The sad truth was that Catherine's dog was better at being hugged than he was at performing tricks, and that was fine with her. Of course, Royce had never appreciated George, and Catherine had even gotten into a fight with her brother over it when he dared laugh at George and say he was part trouble and part horse.

The thought of that argument made Catherine's heart ache. What she would give to have the chance to argue with Royce right now, to see his lazy grin and to hear him call her "Cat." Her throat tightened and tears sprang to her eyes.

As if aware of her thoughts, George lapped her face with a wet tongue.

"Ugh! There's no need for that," Catherine sputtered, wiping her cheek with the back of her hand. A sudden thought occurred. It *was* dangerous traveling alone, and if she couldn't find Derrick in the harbor, it was possible she'd have to find another way to Savannah.

She looked at George. Although she knew he was as dangerous as a sack of wet feathers, he looked like the largest, most ferocious dog to walk the earth. With his huge shaggy head and powerful build, he looked as if he could eat two, maybe three large men.

She took the dog's wide head in her hands and pulled it up until his gaze met hers. "What do you say, old boy? Want to go to Savannah?" George wagged his tail so hard his entire body wagged along with it.

Thus it was that a scant ten minutes later, Catherine and George were on their way to Boston.

CHAPTER TWO

Boston Harbor

"Cap'n, we made good time. We're a good two days early," the first mate said with a touch of pride.

Derrick St. John nodded. "The winds favored us." He looked toward the ocean, admiring the wide lay of the harbor. He'd have just enough time to visit with his mother. He would be glad to see her, even for a few short hours. "As soon as this shipment is unloaded, I'm going ashore."

"Off to see yer mum, eh?" Smythe said. "Give her me best, will ye?"

"Indeed I will. Have the men back on board by dark. If we leave at first light, there's a chance we can make Port Charlotte within two days and fetch the last of the shipment."

Smythe blinked. "By dark? But 'twill take them five or six more hours to unload the casks! That's no time at all."

"We've no choice; we've a shipment to make, and the sooner we get there, the more valuable our haul." Derrick cast a critical gaze over his ship. The *Sea Princess* was his only possession, but she would make his fortune. He watched as his men unloaded the heavy casks of French wine and the crates of carefully wrapped tea. It was a profitable venture. "If we make it back before week's end, I'll reward every sailor with a double portion."

Smythe brightened. "That's generous of ye, Cap'n. 'Tis one of the reasons why the men were so anxious to sign up to sail under yer command. They know of yer reputation."

"It's undeserved," Derrick said shortly. "I demand far more from my men than most other captains."

"Aye, but ye pay them what they're worth and ye treat them with respect. A sailor will weather a thousand storms for a cap'n who'll do so much."

Derrick shrugged off the compliment. "I hate to ask so much from them, but I will not fail, Smythe. I cannot afford to."

The first mate nodded, all three of his chins bobbing. "I know, Cap'n. We'll make it. See if we don't."

Derrick didn't reply.

The wind lifted, bringing the clean scent of the ocean. Derrick lifted his face to the sun and let it warm him. He loved the ocean, and never felt safer or more at home than while sailing.

Most men went to sea to seek their fortunes. Derrick St. John had gone to sea to avoid his. His mother had come from a family not unlike the Markhams, and though she'd married a seafaring man, she'd been determined her son would never step foot on a ship unless it was to travel as a passenger. Derrick's father had agreed, knowing firsthand the hardships to be found at sea. Though the elder St. John was a well respected captain, scandalous accusations threatened his stellar reputation. Thus it was Derrick was sent away to school. He was expected to be a gentleman and to become a banker or a lawyer or some such nonsense.

But Derrick had inherited his father's love of the sea, and he'd fought to be allowed to come home. His parents refused, believing he'd eventually settle in. He didn't; Derrick ran away from school and joined the first ship that would take him, signing on as a cabin boy. The ship set sail for India before his parents realized he was gone.

Life at sea was everything his father had feared—difficult and dangerous. Time and again Derrick cheated death through sheer luck and determination, surviving storms and epidemics and even a pirate attack. Any other boy would have given up and returned home, but not Derrick. He was too proud to give up, too willful to admit he had been wrong. Instead, he forced himself to become tougher, less caring. And he'd never once looked back, surviving each hardship, though the cost was high—very high indeed. Eventually Derrick had forgotten who he was and he fell to the lure of instant riches. He had manned a pirate ship that had preyed along the coast of the Carolinas and relieved many a wealthy merchant ship of its cargo.

Derrick found it exhilarating for a brief time, but he had not thought of all the repercussions. The pirate life palled and soon he found himself a wanted man with a price on his head, unable even to go ashore and visit his parents.

He'd had nowhere to turn. At least that's what he'd thought, until Royce Markham came forward. Royce was a good deal older than Derrick, almost eight years. He was well established in Boston society and very wealthy. He'd respected Derrick's father, always believing in the elder St. John's innocence, and had petitioned the government to issue a pardon for his son.

Derrick never forgot what he owed Royce. They were years apart in age, and stations apart in life, but they shared a love of the sea and the same quick sense of humor. When Royce hired Derrick the day after his pardon was made official, their friendship had been set.

Derrick looked down at his sea-roughened hands where they rested on the smooth wooden railing. "After this voyage, I am releasing the crew."

Smythe made a gulping noise. "Whatever fer? Ye'll never find a more lively crew than this."

"I'm not making any more shipments until I find the man responsible for my father's disgrace. The time has come."

Smythe placed a beefy hand on Derrick's shoulder and

squeezed. "The crew won't desert ye. Most of them sailed with yer father; they'll want to go with ye."

"There won't be any money in it."

"They won't ask fer any. Neither will I."

Derrick looked back out over the ocean. "I'm going to find that devil. See if I don't."

"Ye won't fail, lad. It's not in ye, no more than it was in yer father."

There was a moment of silence and then Derrick faced Smythe with an intent expression. "Father was a good captain, wasn't he?"

"The best I've ever sailed under," Smythe said. "Exceptin' one. Ye've got his gift and a bit more."

"I'm nothing compared to my father."

"That's not true. I've never seen anyone hold a ship like ye do. Yer father would have been proud of ye."

Derrick's jaw tightened. "My father couldn't have been proud of me. I never should have——"

"Ye made some mistakes, laddie," Smythe said almost severely. "Fell into the wrong crowd, ye did. Yer father knew ye'd come around once ye got enough of it."

Derrick gripped the railing tighter. "I wish he'd lived long enough to see that he was right."

"He knows, lad. He was a special man, was yer father. The angels have always been with him. I daresay he's sendin' them yer way even now."

"I don't need angels. All I need is a pistol and the good

fortune to find DeGardineau."

DeGardineau had single-handedly blackened the elder Captain St. John's good name. Of course, no one would have been quite so quick to believe the worst of Captain James St. John had his son not already besmirched the family name with his own nefarious activities.

Derrick rubbed a hand over his eyes, trying to push aside the painful memories. He'd made mistakes and caused both of his parents great pain, but he'd realized his errors and he had the strength to atone for them. That was worth something, surely. But to set everything to rights, he needed to clear his father's name.

Straightening his shoulders, Derrick turned his gaze to the ocean and hoped the weather would continue to favor their journey. Below him, the dock teemed with activity, as sailors, passengers, and tradesmen mingled. Laborers stacked barrels and wooden crates in large, neat piles as the cool ocean breeze wafted the scent of the sea across the narrow line of buildings that rimmed Boston Harbor.

Despite the fact the country was at war, Boston Harbor bustled with life. While there were markedly fewer ships on the sea due to the British patrolling the waters, shipping was still a very profitable industry. Even more so since the war began as people were willing to pay more for the scarce goods that came from overseas.

Derrick managed a faint grin at the thought. Shipping had always been a chancy venture, what with the uncertain weather, the tricky currents of the Atlantic, the number of pirates who preyed on the ships off the coast, and the difficulties of procuring worthwhile merchandise and finding qualified sailors. For someone with Derrick's experience, the new British threat was little more than an added inconvenience to an already difficult chore.

A sudden commotion arose and cries of "Thief!" filled the air. Derrick leaned over the railing and watched as a fat man burst from one of the small taverns, hard on the heels of a lanky boy who looked to be about fourteen.

Despite his girth, the man was fast, but the boy was faster, darting between the milling throngs of people on the wharf.

"He's a fast 'un," Smythe said from where he stood at Derrick's side. The pudgy first mate watched as the boy leaped over a large barrel, much to the dismay of the man chasing him. "Looks as if the lad might get away."

Derrick nodded. The innkeeper was being left farther and farther behind. "He'll make it."

But as soon as he said the words, the innkeeper yelled at two large and burly men, who promptly dropped the barrels they were loading and joined in the chase.

"Uh-oh!" Smythe said, his fat stomach resting on the railing. He shook his head, all three chins wobbling back and forth. "The lad's luck has run out."

Derrick was inclined to agree as he watched the two hefty men dash past the innkeeper and around a stack of barrels. They closed in on the youth, finally cornering him against the wall of an alehouse. The innkeeper caught up and the three men slowly approached the boy. Derrick could hear them mocking the youngster even from that distance.

He frowned. Life on the docks was hard, even more so for a boy on his own.

"'Tis a pity, Cap'n," Smythe said with a sad sigh, "but the docks do tend to attract the lowest forms of humanity."

"Aye," Derrick agreed absently.

"Adventurers, gamblers, and worse. Chances are that boy is indeed a thief."

Derrick didn't care what the boy was, he didn't like the odds—three huge men against a slender youth. It didn't seem fair. The boy crouched lower, his hat pulled forward until his face was hidden, his entire body tensed as if prepared for the worst.

Smythe rubbed a hand across his chin. "I'd say that lad is done for. I wonder if—"

A furry blur of white and russet bounded past the men and planted itself before the boy. Smythe swore, his eyes round. "Saint Peter's bones! What's that? Looks like a horse, it do. But it has no mane."

The men didn't seem to know what the animal was either, for they backed away, their gazes locked on the massive beast.

Derrick squinted against the bright light. He could just

make out the animal's huge head and massive shoulders. *As a matter of fact*, he thought, *that looks just like the dog belonging to—*

"It can't be," he muttered. Frowning, he eyed the ragged boy, who cowered against the wall of the building. Slight of build, he couldn't be more than fourteen . . . or could he?

Derrick examined what he could see of the boy—narrow shoulders beneath a large, loose-fitting coat, long, slender legs encased in worn woollen breeches and delicately thin feet and hands. There was something less than masculine about the line of those legs and the trim curve of the boy's hips.

If Derrick didn't know better, he'd swear he was looking at a girl. A slender girl, rather tall, with long, long legs that—

Catherine Markham. "It can't be!" Derrick pushed away from the railing. There could be no mistaking her. Catherine was the sister of Derrick's best friend, Royce Markham. She was quiet, well-bred, demure—he didn't think he'd heard her say more than ten words the entire time he'd known her. But surely not . . . Catherine Markham wasn't the kind of brazen female to stride about the docks wearing boy's clothing. Surely the lad before him was just a boy and nothing more.

As if in answer to his unspoken question, the "boy" turned toward the dog and a strand of hair escaped the hat. The long tendril curled over one shoulder, glinting gold in the morning light.

Though he couldn't see more than the curve of a chin, Derrick knew exactly what he'd see if the "boy" faced him—an oval face, wide-set green eyes, and a full, soft mouth.

Derrick cursed out loud. What in the world was that blasted girl doing?

"Cap'n, what is it? Ye looks a bit pale. Are ye takin' ill? Must have been the shepherd's pie—"

"I'm not ill," Derrick said shortly, turning from the railing and striding across the deck. "It's that thief."

Smythe trotted behind him, curiosity brightening his watery blue eyes. "The lad? Do ye know him, then?"

"Unfortunately, yes. Stay here, I'll be right back." Derrick bellowed for Lucas as he went. His cabin boy joined him as he took the gangplank in four angry strides and made his way toward the stack of crates where the humongous dog held the sailors at bay.

"What is it, Cap'n?" Lucas asked breathlessly, trying to keep up. His boots clattered on the cobblestones as he scrambled along beside Derrick.

"Trouble," Derrick said shortly. "When I distract the men, grab the boy and hustle him on board the *Sea Princess*. Don't stop for anyone or anything. Do you hear?"

"Aye, Cap'n. We'll run like the wind, we will."

Derrick nodded. It wasn't much of a plan, but it was all he could come up with on such short notice. He made his way down the street as quickly as possible, slowing as he came to the pile of crates. With a stern glance at Lucas, Derrick stepped into the alley where Catherine was being held captive. Her gaze flew to his, her eyes widening with relief when she recognized him.

Derrick gave her a reassuring nod, though he felt more like yelling. What in hell was she thinking? Didn't she realize the danger she'd be in, wandering the docks unprotected? Of course, she probably thought her disguise foolproof, though Derrick had been able to discern that she was a girl from across the entire quay.

Truthfully, the clothing was not much of a disguise. The loose shirt and jacket may have hidden her curves, but the form fitting breeches emphasized her long, feminine legs.

He shot her a glance now, noticing that she seemed pale. Her jaw was set, her eyes smudged with tiredness. A wave of protectiveness rose in him. Usually Catherine looked like the white frosting angel that his mother always put on the top of the Christmas tree: perfectly dressed in an expensive silk gown, her hair arranged in curls, her delicate feet shod in the most expensive slippers.

"Weel, now," one of the burly men said, his red hair matching his torn and dirty shirt. "Who're ye?"

"Derrick St. John, Captain of the *Sea Princess*. I've come for the boy."

The innkeeper snorted. "Ye can't have him. The boy's a thief and he's not going anywhere 'til he's paid fer his supper."

Derrick frowned. "I've come for the lad and I'm not leaving without him."

Lucas tugged on his sleeve. "Cap'n, shall I run back to the ship and gather the men?"

"Ye're not going anywhere." The other man brushed his lank, brown hair out of his eyes and spat onto the cobblestones. Then to Derrick he said, "Ye might be a captain on yer ship, but ye ain't nothin' here."

Catherine looked at Derrick, her green eyes wide. She said his name almost silently, and the faint sound barely reached him.

Derrick forced himself to meet her gaze without response, though his chest tightened. Fear lurked in her eyes, along with genuine relief at his presence. She offered him a tremulous smile, then pushed away the wisps of hair that had escaped her large, floppy hat.

He knew her hair, knew the lush color—a pale golden, like summer honey; the silken strands even now curled around her neck and clung to her collar, reminding him of the last time he'd seen her. Royce had invited Derrick to High Hall for Christmas. As his mother was with family in the country, Derrick had reluctantly agreed.

What Royce had not mentioned was that part of the festivities included a ball. Derrick had been forced to attend and had even danced with some of the young women present—or he had until the whispers began and people realized who he was. He glanced at Catherine and remembered how she'd looked that night, dressed in pink silk, with her hair piled on her head. For the first time, he'd realized that his best friend's little sister was rapidly turning into a beautiful woman.

Derrick grimaced. He shouldn't remember how Catherine looked in her gown. For his own piece of mind, Derrick shouldn't remember anything about Catherine.

She's not for you, he told himself sternly. She was Royce's sister and a member of the wealthiest family in Boston. One day she would marry a man with money and lands. A man who was not the landless son of a supposed traitor.

Her attention flickered past him to the innkeeper and then back. She opened her mouth as if to say something, but Derrick forestalled her with a quick motion of his hand.

"There you are, Royce," Derrick said in a carefully calm tone. "I've been looking all over for you."

The two men pursuing Catherine eyed Derrick suspiciously. "What's the lad to ye?" the largest one asked.

"This is my little brother, Royce," Derrick said smoothly.

"Yer brother, eh?" The man glanced at Catherine. "He don't look like ye much, what with that yaller hair and all."

Derrick shrugged. "He's my half brother, in a way."

"In a way, eh?" The man smirked. "Born on the wrong side of the sheets, eh?"

Catherine stiffened, and Derrick quickly said, "Aye, but he doesn't like us to speak of it."

The other man nodded. As massive as an oak, his thick neck was easily the size of Derrick's thigh. "Brother or no, the lad is a thief." As if to emphasize his words, he took a threatening step forward.

George, alerted by the crunch of the man's boot on the cobblestone walkway, turned immediately, his floppy ears pricked in curiosity.

The man stopped in his tracks, a look of caution on his face. "There, now. I don't like the looks of that animal. He don't bite, do he?"

Derrick glanced at the huge dog. A *real* dog would have stood with teeth bared, ears laid back to ward off an attacker, but George wasn't a real dog. He was an extremely large, overfed stuffed animal, more a pillow with feet than a protector.

But the two men trying to capture Catherine didn't know that. All they saw was a monstrous animal with a massive head and huge jaws filled with glistening teeth.

Derrick managed to swallow a grin as he addressed the man. "I wouldn't move too quickly, if I were you."

At the sound of his voice, George turned toward Derrick. The dog recognized him instantly, and trotted forward, wagging his tail sleepily.

The innkeeper eyed the dog with a mistrustful gaze. "There now, call him off."

Derrick opened his mouth to answer, but before he could speak, George ambled up to him and sank into a large, fluffy puddle on Derrick's boots, almost knocking Derrick off balance.

The red-haired man snorted. "Just look. That dog wouldn't bark at a shadow."

"Stupid mutt," Derrick muttered under his breath. He tried to make George move by lifting the tips of his boots, but the dog just grunted. Why couldn't Catherine have a real dog? One that would protect her? He looked down at George and a sudden thought occurred to him. He looked at the innkeeper and said in a low voice, "Whatever you do, don't move."

The innkeeper frowned. "Why not?"

"Because he always lies down right before he attacks."

"No!" The innkeeper eyed George uneasily. "I can't imagine—"

George lifted his head and looked at the man. The dog's tongue lolled out of his mouth, white bubbles of saliva dripping from the end of it into a little puddle. The sound of his panting filled the air.

The red-haired man shifted, sending an uneasy glance at Derrick. "I say there, mate, do ye think that dog's mad?"

"Lord help us, I hope not," the other man said, backing warily away.

"I don't know," Derrick said thoughtfully. "I've never seen him foam at the mouth before."

Derrick caught Catherine's gaze. She was struggling to contain her laughter. He gave her a warning frown.

"Cap'n?" Lucas said in a low voice, his gaze fastened on the dog. "Should I run to fetch your pistols?"

"Aye," the innkeeper said, brightening up considerably. "That'd take care of this—"

"Wait!" Derrick said, as George tilted up his head and gave a sleepy yawn, a slow line of spittle dripping off his bottom lip.

"What?" the man standing closest to him asked. "What's wrong?"

George wagged his tail and pulled himself to his feet, then stood looking from one man to the next.

"I think he's trying to decide if it's ye he wants or one of us," the smaller of the two men whispered. "I hopes he likes ye better'n me."

The other man swallowed noisily. "W-we could run. Maybe if we walked away real slow-like, the beast wouldn't follow us."

George seemed to think the man was calling him, for he wagged his tail and trotted toward him. Of course, George's idea of a trot was more like a hunchbacked shamble. The man gave a startled shriek, which George decided was a clear invitation to play; he took the last few steps in a large woolly bound. The man whirled around to run, but George followed, managing to lap the man's hand.

"Don't move!" Derrick snapped.

The man froze, one foot in the air. George gave him a puzzled look, though his tail never stopped wagging. Sweat broke out on the man's forehead. He looked at Derrick with a pleading gaze. "He licked my hand first. Do ye think he's seeing if he likes the taste of me?"

Behind him, Derrick heard Catherine stifle a giggle.

"Mortimer," the innkeeper whispered. "Don't ye move a muscle."

Lucas peered around Derrick to where George held the huge man at bay by sitting heavily on his feet. "I've never seen the like," the cabin boy said, clearly awed. "His mouth is big enough to hold me head."

The other large man began to back away.

"Jenkins," Mortimer whispered. "Don't leave me!"

"I'll be back," Jenkins lied, his face pale. "I—I just need to see to me poor ol' mother."

"Yer mother is dead," the innkeeper said sourly. "Instead of runnin' like a fool, why don't ye fetch me blunderbuss from the tavern so we can at least try to save poor ol' Mortimer?"

"Aye!" Jenkins backed up a little quicker now, stumbling for a moment on an uneven cobblestone in the street.

George swung his head at the sound and Jenkins froze, a panicked expression on his face.

"He's onto ye now!" the innkeeper said, pushing his greasy hair from his face with a hand that was none too clean. "I don't like the look in his eyes."

As far as Derrick could tell, the only "look" George had on his furry face was one of an empty-headed dog. But if it kept these hooligans at bay while he helped Catherine to safety, then so be it. He glanced at Catherine and jerked his head, indicating that she was to come to his side.

She did as he requested and once again, he wondered how anyone could think she was a boy—every move she made was unconsciously feminine. Thankfully, the burly men were too busy staring in frightened awe at the "mad" dog to notice anything Catherine did.

"To the ship," Derrick said in a low voice to both Lucas and Catherine.

Lucas pulled his gaze from where George held Mortimer hostage. "Aye, Cap'n! This way!" He grabbed Catherine's arm and pulled her toward the ship.

"Wait," she said, pulling her arm free. "I'm not leaving without George."

"I'll bring him with me," Derrick growled. "Just go!"

"Lord help me," Mortimer groaned, his gaze glued to the dog that sat dripping spittle on his boots. "I've not much in this world, but I cherish me life such as it is."

"Just don't move," Derrick said. He turned toward Catherine and Lucas. "Go."

She didn't like that, he could see it in the downward turn of her lips and the scathing glance she sent him, but he didn't care. So long as she was safe.

Catherine crossed her arms and glared at him. "No. Not without George."

Derrick closed his eyes, his exasperation tightening his jaw. "If you must take that beast, then call him."

She placed her fingers to her lips and gave a shrill whistle.

George raised his head from where he sat on Mortimer's boots and looked at his mistress hopefully.

"He wants more food," Catherine said under her breath. "That's what I was doing in the inn."

"Aye," the innkeeper said, "and that's when ye stole from me."

"I didn't steal anything. I ordered a plate of stew and I left the money on the table."

"So ye say, but I didn't see no coins on the table."

"Was it possible someone else took the money?" Derrick asked.

The innkeeper frowned as if that thought hadn't occurred to him. "I suppose that could have happened. But that don't matter. Any fool knows not to just lay their money on the table and walk off."

Catherine's face reddened, but she didn't say anything. Instead, she gave another whistle, this one louder than the first. George responded this time, padding to her side with a lumbering grace.

"Praise Saint Peter." Mortimer sighed, sagging against the stack of barrels. "Me life flashed before me eyes when that beast looked at me."

"Lucas," Derrick said. "Escort my brother and his beast to the ship."

"Aye, Cap'n!" Lucas stood aside for Catherine, making sure the dog was on her other side, as far away from him as possible.

Catherine made as if to protest, but one look at Derrick's face and she clamped her mouth closed and followed Lucas back into the street, George close on her heels.

It was with relief that Derrick saw the three of them disappear among the swarm of merchants and seamen who crowded the docks. The innkeeper began to complain loudly of his lost money and Derrick poured enough coins in the man's hands that he finally left, Mortimer trailing behind, still looking nervously over his shoulder is if expecting George to return.

"What a mess," Derrick muttered as he made his way back toward the *Sea Princess*. What on earth was Catherine Markham doing here, on the docks, dressed as a boy?

Whatever the reason, Derrick had a feeling he wasn't going to like it. He'd get some decent clothing for Catherine and send her home as soon as he could. Royce would be worried to death if he found out his sister wasn't safely at home.

Derrick wondered how long Catherine had been gone. His footsteps slowed . . . something didn't add up.

Whatever it was, he'd find out as soon as he got to the *Sea Princess*.

Stifling a sigh, Derrick merged into the crowd and made his way back to his ship.

CHAPTER THREE

Derrick found Catherine and Lucas on the dock, admiring the *Sea Princess* while George sat panting at Catherine's feet, his eyes closed as if he anticipated falling asleep at any moment. Catherine stared up at the tall masts overhead, long wisps of hair spilling down her back, the golden strands bright against her dark coat.

Lucas talked loudly, his young voice brimming with enthusiasm as he described the various features of the ship. "'Tis a grand ship, she is. Square rigged and as right as they come. Ye should have seen her when we engaged a pirate ship outside of—Oh! There ye are, Cap'n," Lucas said, grinning from ear to ear. "Miss Markham was admirin' the *Sea Princess*."

Derrick raised a brow. "*Miss* Markham?"

"He figured out I wasn't a boy," she said, still looking up at the mast, her hat shadowing her face from the sun. "Lucas, have you really climbed all the way to the top?"

"Aye, miss. I've climbed it many a time when on watch. Ye can see fer miles and miles from up there."

Her gaze softened as she looked up, a faraway expression in her eyes. "Miles and miles," she murmured softly. "Is it frightening?"

"Only the first time. After that—" He shrugged. "Ye get used to it."

"I don't think I'd ever get used to that." She smiled dreamily. "Still, I'd like to climb to the top one day."

Lucas pursed his lips. "'Tis a dangerous thing, to be climbin' the rigging. I've seen many a man fall to his death."

Derrick couldn't believe that the usually prim, proper Catherine was standing on the dock, having a conversation with a common cabin boy about the thrills of climbing the ship's rigging. This was not the Catherine Markham he knew.

"It's time to go aboard," Derrick said shortly. He'd had enough of Catherine for one day. He'd send word to Royce that he'd found his wayward sister and then send her back to High Hall, where she belonged. "Miss Markham, allow me to see you to my cabin."

She pulled her gaze from the rigging with obvious reluctance. "Thank you. I must speak with you."

Derrick cast a quick glance at Lucas, who stood watching them with a speculative look, as if he was working something out for himself. "Go aboard and tell Smythe we've a visitor."

"Aye, Cap'n." Lucas grinned merrily at Catherine and then he was off, dashing up the gangway, his spindly legs flashing.

Catherine watched him go, her heart sinking in her

chest. For some reason, she was nervous, her stomach tied in knots. She was unaccustomed to feeling powerless, but she *had* to have Derrick's help if she was to succeed in rescuing Royce. She'd spent the entire journey to the harbor thinking of what she'd say to Derrick, but now words failed her.

Perhaps her nerves were caused by the fact that Derrick looked different here, at the dock. He was in command, but he also appeared older than when he'd come to visit Royce at High Hall. Of course, it had been some months since she'd seen him and she couldn't help but notice that his shoulders were broader, though his dark hair was shorter.

She glanced at him and then quickly away. Derrick St. John was far too handsome for her peace of mind. She cleared her throat. "Your cabin boy seems to know the ship quite well," Catherine remarked, trying to find something to say to ease the tension that threatened to strangle her voice.

"You should see him climb the rigging," Derrick replied. "He's like a monkey."

Catherine nodded, then tried to think of something funny or halfway intelligent to add, but all she could come up with was, "How did you escape that horrid innkeeper? I suppose he was difficult."

"I paid him."

"You *what*?" Her hands went to her hips. "Please don't tell me that bully forced you into giving him even more money! I already paid him once, and far more than I should have." That much was true—all she'd had with her were the gold pieces from the secret compartment and, though she'd been loath to part with one, she hadn't thought she could very well leave the inn without paying.

"I had to do something, Catherine. The man believed you hadn't paid him at all."

"Well, I did," Catherine said hotly. George seemed to hear the anger in her voice, for he lifted his head and looked at her with a quizzical gaze, his head cocked to one side.

Catherine just wished Derrick was as nice as her dog. Instead of offering his sympathy, he stood before her, arms crossed over his chest, a faint hint of annoyance in his gaze, as if he thought she was but a small yet annoying occurrence in his rather busy day.

And that was something Catherine was quite unused to. At High Hall, whenever she had something to say, people listened, whether it was one of the servants, or Royce, or even Uncle Elliot. They might not agree with her, but they never made her feel as if she was a fool. "I'll have you know, Mr. Derrick St. John, that I am a Markham. Markhams do not steal."

Derrick just shrugged, an infuriating smile touching his lips. "I know exactly what you are. I am well acquainted with your family." His gaze flickered across her. "I'm not likely to forget them."

Something washed over Catherine and suddenly the events of the last twenty-four hours tumbled in on her. She was tired and hungry and afraid. What had seemed like the simplest of plans had proven far more formidable than she'd thought.

The escape from High Hall had gone easily enough, but the trip to the harbor had been fraught with more dangers than she'd imagined. Since she'd never traveled to the harbor except by carriage, she'd grossly misjudged the distance. She'd thought it would take only a brisk four-hour walk, but instead it had taken almost twice that. And since she'd left in the late afternoon, darkness fell before she could even see the lights of the harbor.

There was no moon, either, and travel after dark was too dangerous to contemplate, so Catherine was forced to find shelter. She stumbled along the road, the too-large boots rubbing her heels and making her progress that much slower, finally settling on a large barn in the middle of a field.

George didn't make things any easier. His large size frightened the dozing cows that filled the pasture and he showed an alarming tendency to want to run after every chicken that sat roosting in the dark corners of their temporary shelter. It took Catherine the better part of an hour to settle him down.

She awoke the next morning to face an angry farmer who roughly demanded to know who she was. Startled from a deep sleep, Catherine hadn't been able to find her voice enough to answer and she scrambled to her feet and ran, George loping after her. After that, she made it to town only to realize that, though the bag of gold was still securely tied to her waist, she'd left her bundle of supplies in the hay pile.

Arriving in town did nothing to soothe her tattered nerves. Boston was a bustling place. Like all other growing cities, it was large and noisy and smelly, especially compared to life in the country at High Hall. Catherine had been to Boston many other times, usually to shop while Royce did business at the dock. But it was different arriving in a carriage and staying at the finest posting houses while surrounded by a barrage of servants. Catherine had never realized how big the city was, or how unfriendly it could be to someone arriving on foot with nothing more than a large, furry animal.

She'd made her way to the harbor only to find no ships that she recognized among the ones tied at the docks. It had taken all of her determination not to turn back then and there. Despondent, Catherine had gone into one of the less dirty inns along the waterfront and ordered a plate of whatever was hot. The slovenly barmaid had just plunked a plate of greasy-looking stew in front of Catherine when she looked out the window and caught sight of the *Sea Princess* tying up at the dock.

A stab of pure, unrelenting hope had warmed her and

she'd hastily taken one bite of the stew before she set the plate on the floor for George, who slurped it up. Then she'd tossed a coin onto the table and left, her entire attention focused on reaching Derrick's ship.

Until the innkeeper began to chase her, that was. Catherine brushed her hand over her eyes. Here she was, so tired she could barely keep her eyes open, so hungry it felt as if it had been weeks since her last meal, and so frightened that she would fail to reach Royce in time that she could barely keep tears from her eyes. *Please God, let me succeed.*

Forcing her lips into a straight line, she stuffed her hands in her pockets to hide the fact that they shook. Everything would be well now that she had found Derrick. He would assist her, she just knew it. But for some reason, she couldn't make her lips form the question.

Perhaps it was the realization that if he refused, she was lost. Perhaps it was because he was so handsome she found it difficult to form sentences around him.

The thought made her scowl. He'd always had that effect on her, though she'd done her best to hide it. He was her brother's friend, four years older than she and he had never even noticed that she was alive. Which was for the best, Catherine decided, lifting her chin. She wouldn't have had it any other way.

She glanced at him now. In his black pants and loose white shirt, his face darkened with a day's growth of stubble, he looked like a pirate. A very handsome, rakish pirate. But Derrick St. John no longer sailed the seas as an outlaw, as he'd once done. He sailed now as the captain of his own ship.

George rose and ambled toward Derrick. Catherine frowned. "George, come!"

George didn't even look at her. He reached Derrick, lifted his muzzle, and slavered his long wet tongue across the back of Derrick's hand.

"Hey!" Derrick yanked his hand out of the way and then wiped it on his pants. He scowled at Catherine. "Can't you train him not to do that?"

"I've tried. He won't listen to anyone but Royce." At the mention of her brother, her throat tightened painfully. At this very moment, Royce could be injured or starving. . . . Catherine pressed a hand to her stomach and tried to stop the tears from welling up in her eyes.

"What is it?" Derrick asked, his brows lowered as he noticed her expression. He took a quick step to her side. "Catherine, why are you here alone? Where's Royce? He would never allow you to roam the docks dressed like that."

Here was her chance. Catherine took a deep breath. "Derrick, I need your help. Royce . . ." The words caught in her throat and swelled.

"Royce what?" Derrick frowned. "Catherine, what's happened?"

"Royce . . . he's gone."

"What?" Derrick paled. "Gone? He isn't—"

"No!" she said quickly. "He's not dead, if that's what you're thinking. At least, I don't think he is, though Uncle Elliot believes otherwise."

Derrick's brow lowered, his color returning. "Your uncle thinks Royce is dead? Catherine, explain."

"Someone has captured Royce. I must get to Savannah by the first of June or they'll . . ." She swallowed, a lump as big as a ship swelling in her throat. "Royce needs us, Derrick. We have to reach Savannah."

He had a hundred questions to ask—she could see it in his face. But now was not the time, nor the place. She glanced nervously over her shoulder, scanning the milling crowd for her uncle, but she saw nothing—not yet, anyway. But it was only a matter of time before Uncle Elliot showed up. "Derrick, I—I could use something to eat. Please."

He raked a hand through his hair, his face lined with conflict. After a long moment, he gave a nod. "Cook made some shepherd's pie. It isn't what you're used to, but it will fill you up."

Her stomach rumbled at the thought of food although she managed a faint smile. "I'm so hungry, I could eat a horse."

Derrick's face softened, the lines about his mouth easing somewhat. "Come on, then. Let's get some food into you. But once you've eaten, I want to know everything that has happened."

"That sounds fair." Catherine whistled at George, who

had dropped back into a lump of relaxed dog at her feet, and then she allowed Derrick to escort her up the steep walkway, the dog's nails clicking on the wood behind them.

As they walked, she tried to focus on the present. If she thought of the last few days, she might dissolve into tears. And if she thought of the future, her fear for Royce would keep her from being able to explain why she thought her brother was in danger.

To keep her mind clear, she instead paid attention to the ship and her surroundings. She had always loved the smell of the docks. She wasn't sure if it was the heady smell of pitch mingled with the salty tang of the ocean, or the mixture of spices that came from the splintered crates that lined the harbor, but it always made her take long, deep breaths, as if she could taste each and every exotic scent.

She stepped onto the deck and noted the clean and polished surface. Royce had always said Derrick ran a tight, well-ordered ship. Having seen him bark orders, Catherine could believe it. She stole a glance at Derrick and wondered at the solemn look on his face. It was as if the second he stepped on deck, he became more focused somehow.

"I haven't seen your ship before," she said, looking around uneasily. "It's larger than Royce had described."

"The *Sea Princess* is one of the first of her kind." A quiet pride resonated in his voice. "She dances lightly through the waves, can carry a double allotment of cargo, and can sail through a storm unlike any ship I've been on."

"She's beautiful," Catherine murmured, and meant it. The *Sea Princess* stood out among the other ships that were docked at harbor—it was more than the impressive heights of the mast or her graceful lines. It was the way every plank and brass fitting had been polished until it shone, each rope was neatly coiled or tied, and the way even the barrels on the deck were arranged in a neat line. The other ships looked messy and unkempt in comparison.

A round, portly man scurried up to Derrick as soon as they were aboard. "There ye be, Cap'n!" the man called, his gaze fixed first on Catherine and then on George with equal curiosity. "Have ye a new recruit? And a dog, too! 'Tis a special day fer us all, eh?"

"I wouldn't call either a pleasant discovery," Derrick said. "More like a barnacle that we'll have to scrape off the ship."

Catherine glanced up at him. "What's that supposed to mean?"

"Lord love ye!" the round man exclaimed at the sound of her voice, his gaze widening. "'Tis not a lad at all! 'Tis a . . ." He looked around, then whispered, "'Tis a wench!"

"So she is. Smythe, let me introduce you to Miss Catherine Markham, sister of Royce Markham and the source of the trouble on the dock this morning. Catherine, this is Smythe, my first mate. He sailed with my father before me."

"'Tis a pleasure to meet ye, miss." Smythe made a ponderous show of bowing, one arm before him in an attempt to be gentlemanly. George took this as an invitation to make himself known and he stuck his wet muzzle into the first mate's palm.

"Ugh!" Smythe jerked upright and wiped his hand on his pants. "That animal licked me."

"George was only saying hello," Catherine said, her face red. "He, um, he's not very well trained."

"Indeed," Derrick said, frowning at the dog.

"I hope ye don't mind me mentionin' it, miss," Smythe said, "but that's a big dog fer a dab of a gal like ye."

Catherine drew herself up. It was annoying to be called a "dab" of anything. "I'm almost as tall as Clarissa Carlton, and she is two years older than I."

Derrick frowned. "Who is Clarissa Carlton?"

"The redhead you danced with the last time you visited." Clarissa, the toast of Boston, was not only red-headed, but tall, with creamy white skin. Up until that particular party, Catherine had also thought Clarissa a fairly nice person.

To her chagrin, Catherine remembered every moment Derrick had danced around the room, Clarissa's red hair bright against the black of his coat. "You cannot have forgotten Clarissa. She's a bit too tall and always wears the most atrocious blue gowns."

Derrick grinned, his teeth flashing white against his tanned skin. "I don't remember a redhead in a blue gown. But I do remember a blonde in a pink gown."

Catherine immediately began reviewing every woman who had been at the ball. Who had worn a pink gown? She rapidly reviewed her friends and their wardrobes. Marian Blakely owned a pink gown, but Catherine was almost certain Marian had worn her green silk for the occasion. Perhaps he was talking about Sara Lawton, who owed several pink gowns, all of them so low cut that Catherine thought it was only a matter of time before she popped out of one in public.

Derrick looked at her, a quizzical gleam in his gaze. "You wore a pink gown, Catherine. Don't you remember?"

Catherine's cheeks flushed and she found she could only stammer a lame "Oh." She *had* worn a pink gown, hadn't she? A strange warmth filled her at the realization that Derrick had noticed her more than she'd thought.

The first mate beamed at her pleasantly. "'Tis nice of ye to visit us, miss. Would ye like a tour o' the ship?"

"Not now," Derrick said. "Miss Markham and I have some matters to discuss."

Disappointment colored the first mate's round face, but he managed to swallow it. "Perhaps later, then."

"I'd like that," Catherine said, smiling. Perhaps her worries were over. She'd made it to Derrick's ship and her uncle had not yet tracked her down. All she had to do was explain to Derrick exactly what had happened to Royce and they'd be on their way to Savannah within the hour. Her heart eased a bit.

"Smythe, have Cook send some food to my cabin for Miss Markham. She's hungry."

"Not the shepherd's pie," Smythe said, sending Catherine a warning glance. "'Tis not the kind of fare a lady would enjoy."

Derrick shot a frown at his first mate. "Shepherd's pie will do, so long as it's warm."

Smythe nodded and then scuttled off, humming to himself as he went.

"This way," Derrick said, crossing the deck toward a small door.

Catherine followed, watching him duck his head and make his way into the ship down a dark and narrow corridor. They walked the length of the hallway, George hard on her heels, before Derrick stopped at a door that was larger than the others. He pushed it open, then stood aside.

Catherine stepped inside and came to an abrupt halt. "I can't believe this is inside a ship." And she couldn't. The room was surprisingly large and spacious. A heavy table held precedence in the center of the room, surrounded by impressive, carved chairs. A desk rested against one wall, beneath a wide assortment of portholes and windows.

A wide bunk was built into one wall, hung with red

curtains that echoed the color of the plump cushions on the seats and the drapes that framed the windows. A thick rug adorned the floor and a number of gleaming brass lanterns were fastened to the walls. "Are the other cabins this nice?"

"No. They are quite a bit smaller." He gestured to a chair at the table. "Explain what has happened to Royce."

Catherine slid into a chair, noticing that it was fastened to the floor. George plopped at her feet with a grateful sigh and rolled onto his side, falling into a deep slumber almost immediately.

Now that she was here, safely ensconced in Derrick's cabin, his full attention on her, Catherine didn't know where to begin. After a moment's struggle, she said, "I didn't thank you for helping me. I don't know what I would have done if you hadn't arrived."

"It was nothing." Derrick took the seat opposite hers, his gaze resting on her hands.

Catherine realized she was gripping the edge of the table so tightly that her knuckles were white. She released the table and took a calming breath. What if he didn't believe her? What if he thought she was overreacting— that Uncle Elliot was right about the note? That it was a trick and that Royce really was . . . she caught her breath, a heavy weight pressing against her chest. She would not believe that Royce was gone forever.

"Catherine, what's happened?" Derrick's voice was

deep with concern. "Where's Royce?"

She took a calming gulp of air. "Two weeks ago, Royce left Boston Harbor with a shipment. He was returning when . . ." She straightened her shoulders. "The ship was attacked by a British vessel. Some of the crew . . . they said Royce was knocked into the ocean when the mast fell."

Derrick paled as he sat back in his chair. "So he's dead."

"No!" The word was both a cry and a denial.

"Catherine, I don't understand. I thought you said—"

"They're wrong! I know it!" Her lips quivered and she had to blink away the tears. "He's not dead. This may sound strange, but I can feel that he is still alive. I just know he is."

"Do you have any proof that he is alive other than your feelings?"

"Yes. There's one more thing."

"What?"

"A note. I found it on the desk in the library. It was a ransom note. Derrick, they . . . they say they have Royce captive and they will exchange him for gold. If we don't deliver the money, they will kill him."

Derrick's mouth thinned. "Do you know who this 'they' are?"

She shook her head. "The note didn't say. I don't understand why they would do this."

"Your brother is a wealthy man. That's reason enough

for some men. How much gold do they want?"

"Fifty pieces."

He gave a low whistle. "That's a fortune."

"I have more than enough. Derrick, the money must be delivered to Savannah in less than two weeks." She leaned forward, her heart in her eyes. "Will you help me?"

Derrick's gaze locked with hers. "Of course, I'll help you. In fact, I'll deliver the money to Savannah myself."

CHAPTER FOUR

Catherine jumped to her feet and threw her arms around Derrick's neck in an impulsive hug. "Oh, thank you! I knew you would help!"

Derrick didn't move. In his wildest dreams, he'd never imagined calm, cool Catherine Markham actually touching him. He stayed completely still, aware of the silky feel of her hair against his cheek, of the warmth of her arms about his neck.

She released him all too quickly and sat back down, her face alive with happiness. "We can leave at once and—"

"Wait. Catherine, there are things I need to know first. What exactly did this note say?"

Her brow creased and she said slowly, as if remembering each word, "It said that they had captured Royce and if the Markham family wanted to see him again, that they would bring fifty gold pieces to Savannah."

"Did it mention a specific location?"

"Yes, the Red Rooster Inn."

Derrick nodded absently as he assessed his options. When all Derrick had seen before him was a life of thievery and shame, Royce Markham had been the one to prove him wrong. He'd offered Derrick employment when no one else would, and had trusted him implicitly. And Derrick had returned the favor by becoming the most trustworthy captain in Royce's fleet.

In many ways, Royce Markham was the brother Derrick never had. Derrick would have walked across hot coals to help him, no matter the cost.

"I owe Royce more than I can say." And he'd repay that debt by going after him—and taking care of his younger sister in the meantime. Derrick looked across the table at Catherine, noticing again the tiredness beneath her happy glow, and the faint circles under her eyes. "How did you get to Boston?"

"I walked." She smiled rather weakly. "And walked. And walked."

"All the way from High Hall? That's miles away."

She grimaced down at her dusty boots. "I have blisters on my feet to prove it."

"Why didn't you just take one of your carriages?"

Catherine pulled her hat off her head and placed it on the table in front of her. More strands of golden hair had escaped her ribbon and softly framed her face. "I was afraid to take a carriage because Uncle Elliot might have tried to stop me."

"Your uncle is at High Hall?"

Catherine nodded. "He came as soon as he heard

about Royce. He thinks the ransom note is a fake and I didn't have time to try and convince him otherwise. He's not a person who changes his mind very easily."

Having met Catherine's uncle, Derrick could easily believe that. The man was cold, as controlled as a snake. "So you made your way here, without any protection."

"I had George."

"Like I said, you made your way here, without any protection."

Catherine's lips quivered on the verge of a smile. "George would have protected me, had there been any danger."

Derrick looked down at the dog that lay snoring on the floor. The huge mutt was lying on his back, his feet splayed in the air, his ears flat on the floor about his head. Derrick snorted. "That mutt is as much protection as a broken butter churn. Catherine, I don't approve of what you did—it was dangerous, with or without that mutt, but . . ."

"But?" Her green eyes glittered a challenge.

He smiled gently. "I'm glad you came to me."

After an astonished moment, she smiled. "Me too. Derrick, we have less than two weeks to reach Savannah. I thought perhaps we should—"

"'We'?" he interrupted. "I never said we were going to Savannah. I will go to Savannah. You will stay here with my mother until—"

"You can't mean that!" Catherine flushed a deep red, her mouth forming a straight line. "Royce is my brother, Derrick. I am going with you."

"No, you're not," Derrick returned just as firmly. "It will be dangerous. The British are out there, as are a whole horde of pirates and all sorts of other dangers. I won't have you risk your life."

"I am not a child."

No, she wasn't. The fact that she'd managed to make it as far as she had without detection was proof of that. "I know that. You are a lady, and Royce wouldn't want you to—"

"Royce would do the same for me or you. You know that."

"Catherine, be reasonable. I can't take you and—"

She picked up her hat and stood. "If you won't take me, than I'll convince someone else to do it. There are other ships and I have enough gold to buy my passage."

Derrick could see the determination that shone in her eyes. "Sit down."

"The *Sea Princess* isn't the only ship out there. I can—"

"Catherine," Derrick snapped. "Sit. Down."

She dropped back into her chair, her cheeks hot, her eyes flashing defensively. "I'm going with you whether you want me to or not."

Royce raked a hand through his hair. This situation was difficult enough without having to deal with Catherine's presence on board ship. But she was right—there were other ships and he had little doubt that if she flashed enough gold, one of them would take her wherever she wanted. Which would mean she would arrive in Savannah unprotected. *If* she even made it to Savannah. Sailors were a curious lot, respectful toward some women and disrespectful toward others. And in his life at sea, Derrick had seen it all. "Very well. I'll take you."

Catherine couldn't quite swallow, but she managed a husky murmur: "You . . . you will?"

"Yes," he returned grimly. "But only on the condition that you do as I say. I cannot rescue Royce if I have to worry about you."

"I want to help too."

"You can help by staying on board ship when we reach Savannah. Catherine, can you at least promise me you'll do that much?"

She toyed with the brim of the hat that sat on the table before her, her gaze haunted. After a long moment, she shook her head, the movement loosening even more wisps of hair. "I can't promise such a thing and you know it."

Derrick saw the determination in the set of her shoulders. This was not the Catherine Markham he knew—not that he'd known her all that well before. He'd thought she was a cosseted, protected female more interested in the number of ribbons she wore than anything else. He'd been wrong. Catherine Markham loved her brother deeply and it was apparent she would walk through fire to save his life, with or without Derrick's help.

He closed his eyes and wondered what ill fate had forced this situation. He had no choice. He sighed loudly. "Oh, very well. You may come. We'll discuss how best to handle Savannah when we reach port."

She smiled then, a brilliant flash of white teeth. "Thank you!"

"Thank me after we have Royce alive and well. I suppose we should write your uncle a note and let him know you are safe."

Her fingers tightened about the hatband. "I'd rather not."

"Why not?"

"He would try to stop us, since he thinks it is madness to pay the ransom."

"I can see why. Catherine, it is a very real possibility that these people don't have Royce and are just trying to trick you."

She stopped fidgeting with her hat long enough to meet Derrick's gaze, her eyes dark with concern. "I know. I—I'm prepared to deal with that fact if we discover it is true. But we have to try."

He nodded absently. Something didn't add up. Derrick wasn't sure what it was, but it would come to him. He wondered briefly if perhaps Catherine's uncle had other reasons for not wanting the gold delivered to the kidnappers, but after a moment's thought, he shrugged the idea aside. If anyone stood to benefit from Royce's death, it would be Catherine and not her uncle.

Meanwhile, Derrick had much to do if he was to depart for Savannah with the tide. He needed to send word to his mother and let her know his visit was to be delayed. And he'd need to send a letter to the East India Tea Company to let them know that he would be late in arriving to pick up the last shipment. He could only hope they wouldn't hire out another ship to do the job. Royce was far more important to him than making a shipment, however.

A rapid knock sounded on the door. Derrick called a greeting and first mate Smythe entered followed by Little, who served as cook.

The wiry, thin cook held a platter of steaming food in one hand, a wide pewter plate in the other. "I've brought some vittles fer the young lady." He placed the plate on the table with a flourish. Then he set the platter beside Catherine and removed the cover.

A black nose appeared at the edge of the table as George made his presence known, sniffing loudly.

"George!" Catherine admonished. "You may have some when I finish."

He sighed heavily and rested his chin on her knee, looking soulfully at the underside of the table.

Derrick watched as Catherine leaned forward to capture the rich smell of shepherd's pie. Most of her hair had escaped the ribbon that held it back. The long golden tendrils clung to the rough coat she wore. Derrick frowned. She would need some decent clothing before they left port.

Catherine didn't seem to care. "I'm starving," she said, picking up the fork that Little magically produced from one of his pockets. She took a huge bite and closed her eyes, a blissful expression on her face.

"Aye," Smythe said with a frown. "Tastes like heaven, which is why I don't trust it. We've never had a cook who could make food taste like *that*."

"I'm a genius," Little said, smiling graciously. "No one cooks the way I can."

"Smythe," Derrick said. "Miss Markham needs appropriate clothing. There is a shop off the quay where one can purchase ladies' things. Could you see what they have for her?"

The first mate sized Catherine up. She blushed and said, "No, that's not necessary. I can——"

"Aye, Cap'n," Smythe said cheerfully. "I'll take care of it meself."

"Excellent," Derrick said, jerking his head toward the door. "That will be all."

Both men bowed to Catherine, then left, stopping in the hallway to argue over the likelihood of Little's being the best cook to ever grace a ship's galley. Their voices lingered in the hallway for several long moments, but Catherine didn't notice, she was far too busy eating.

Derrick watched with satisfaction as she ate. She hadn't been teasing when she'd said she was starving—she was already on her second helping of the shepherd's pie. When she finished, she heaped a mound on her plate and set it on the floor in front of George, who attacked it with a half growl.

Restless, Derrick rose and went to a small stand beside the bunk and poured a measure of water into a cup. "You're lucky I was in port—I wasn't scheduled to arrive for two more days, but we had some favorable winds." He brought the cup to the table and handed it to Catherine.

"If you weren't here, I'd have bought passage on another ship. I have money." She patted her pocket and broke into a sudden grin. "More than enough."

Her confidence surprised him, and for some reason irritated him. "It's not that easy to find passage. This country is at war. The British have imposed a blockade and they are doing their best to sink every American ship they can find."

"I know," she replied. "But this is important. Derrick, if we don't deliver the gold in ten days, they will harm Royce. He's in far more danger than we'll be."

Derrick knew he should have made her stay behind. But somehow, looking into her pleading green eyes, Derrick heard himself say, "We'll leave on the evening tide."

"With your help, everything will work out. I know it will!" George finished eating and laid his muzzle on

Catherine's arm. She hugged him and chuckled. "Did you hear that, George? We're going to Savannah!"

"Wonderful. I get to travel with a mutt the size of a barn," Derrick said, feeling as if he had to regain control in some way. "He will have to stay down in the hold."

"But . . . won't it be dark?"

"You can visit him whenever you like."

Her arms tightened about the creature's neck. "George is afraid of the dark! We can't put him down there."

"Well, I cannot have a dog as big as a horse wandering the decks. It could cause all sorts of problems."

"Like what?"

Derrick scowled. "I don't know—just problems."

Catherine scratched George's ear, grinning at him when he made a little whirring sound deep in his throat. After the harrowing trip she and George had just made, she wasn't about to leave him in a cold, dark hold. "Don't worry about George; I'll keep him with me, in my cabin."

Derrick leaned back in his chair and looked at her for a long moment, his blue eyes showing his amusement. "You are incorrigible."

"Perhaps. But I'm not as bad as Royce."

Derrick didn't answer, but remained where he was, leaning back in his chair, one arm resting on the table, his gaze fastened on her.

"What?" she finally said, agonizingly aware of his gaze. He made her feel uncomfortable just by looking at her.

"What does your uncle stand to gain if your brother disappears? *You* would inherit everything, not him."

Catherine blinked at the sudden question. What was Derrick talking about?

"Well?" Derrick asked. He crossed his arms over his chest, and regarded her with a serious gaze. The indirect light that shone from the porthole made his eyes look almost black, the lashes casting shadows across his cheeks.

"Uncle Elliot won't inherit anything. He will be the executor of the estate, though." She frowned. She hadn't thought of that before.

Derrick's face darkened. "Catherine, you don't seem to understand how serious this is. Perhaps you'd *like* to see your Uncle Elliot in possession of High Hall and the Markham Tea Company?"

"And perhaps you'd *like* a black eye," she retorted.

Derrick grinned. "You couldn't reach my eye. Either of them."

"I can now," she said, lifting her chin. It was true. Though Derrick was tall, so was she. She practically towered over all her friends, a fact that made her feel awkward and uncertain. Her friend Marian, for example, was a tiny thing with a head full of golden curls and a rounded figure that made Catherine feel positively flat. The boys fell over themselves to win a smile from Marian, while they tended to ignore Catherine.

She glanced at Derrick from beneath her lashes. She

realized she was fighting to prove herself as much as he was. Of course, she didn't have so much to overcome. She tried to remember what little she'd heard about Derrick's past. Royce had told her some details, but it was quickly becoming obvious that he hadn't told her all of it. She squared her shoulders and said, "Perhaps this journey will be a test."

He lifted a brow. "A test of what?"

"Derrick, I know you've been working hard to prove yourself after your father . . ." What had Royce told her? Catherine struggled to remember it all. Something about abandoning his ship to the British? Was that it?

Derrick's face closed. "My father is not a part of this."

"I know," she said quickly, feeling as if she was bungling everything. "But this is an opportunity to make good. I know Royce believed in you, and I believe in you, too."

Derrick's mouth softened into a slight smile. "Don't throw your wiles at me. I'm immune. I've already said I'd help. You had just better hope your uncle doesn't catch up to us, or we'll both be in trouble. He's within his legal rights to demand that you return home."

She sniffed. "He has no legal rights where I am concerned."

"He does if your brother left you to his care."

"Nonsense. I am perfectly able to take care of myself."

"Catherine, the *Sea Princess* is a blockade runner. The British are out there, looking for our ships—with cannons, guns, and whatever ill weapon they have. They'd like to see us all at the bottom of the sea, and they will take great pains with their efforts to do just that." Derrick shook his head. "I'm a fool to take you with me and if I didn't think you'd just find another ship, one less able to reach Savannah safely, I'd pick you up, toss you over my shoulder, and take you home myself."

"I'm not afraid."

"You should be."

"Derrick, I am seventeen years old and this is a decision I've made. *We* will go in search of my brother and *we* will bring him back."

Derrick's gaze darkened. "I don't want you in danger. Royce would never forgive me if something happened to you."

"You might be able to stop me from going to Savannah on the *Sea Princess*, but you can't stop me from going to Savannah on another ship."

A slow smile touched his mouth and Catherine couldn't look away. "Don't tempt me, sweetheart," he said, his voice low and menacing.

Catherine's nails curled into her palms. "I am *not* your sweetheart."

His gaze flickered over her face. After a moment, he shrugged. "We are getting nowhere with this." He stood, his head barely clearing the ceiling. "We'll discuss what's to be done about Savannah once we've left port. The rest of the men will return at nightfall and we can get under way then. In the meantime, I'm going to check to see if we've restocked our supplies."

Catherine stood as well, feeling the need to do something useful. "Derrick, I . . . thank you. No matter what happens, you have already proven yourself a true friend. To both Royce and me."

Derrick stood still, looking down at her, a heated expression in his eyes. A slow tingle traveled through Catherine at that look, as if it had been an actual touch.

He turned abruptly and went to the door. "Wait here. I'll send someone to take you to your cabin."

Catherine started to ask if she could go up on deck too, but Derrick didn't give her the chance. The door was closing behind him before she could even form the words.

She slowly sank back in her chair, absently patting George when the dog rested his damp chin on her knee. "Well," she said aloud to no one in particular. "I think that went well."

CHAPTER FIVE

Elliot Markham stood at the library window of High Hall and watched the last of the sun's rays sparkle across the water. One of the things he liked best about High Hall was that it stood on a large graceful hill that gently sloped down to the cold lap of Boston Harbor, separated from the ocean by a wide section of rocky beach. The views from the house were exquisite.

The mansion itself was large and elegant, made of luxurious pink stone imported from some distant land. Filled with leaded glass windows and gleaming wood floors, it held treasures in every corner. Fireplaces of Italian marble, delicate crystal chandeliers, ornate iron scrolling over the doorways—every hallway was covered with thick, lush rugs.

Elliot turned away from the sun and returned to his desk. He stopped for a moment . . . no, it wasn't his desk. Not yet, anyway.

Life had never favored Elliot as it had his brother, John, a truth that made Elliot's stomach sour. He sat down in the large leather chair and turned so that he could look back out to where the harbor glistened in the late afternoon sun.

Few homes could boast the creature comforts found at High Hall, a fact that made Elliot's life seem even less satisfactory than it already was. He should have been happy in these peaceful hours before dark, but the knowledge that the desk before him, the Persian rug beneath his feet, and even the mahogany chair beneath his rump, all belonged to someone else gave Elliot no pleasure at all. What he wanted was wealth. Power. The comfort of knowing he was better than everyone else and having the lifestyle that proved it.

But fate had somehow denied him the success that should have been his. And for that, he was bitter. Bitter and angry. Life was unfair, and it was even more unfair that Elliot should spend his entire life watching as all the things he craved fell neatly into his brother's lap. He'd become so bitter that he hadn't even been able to summon a single tear when John had been killed.

Fortunately, there was more than one way to gain one's place in the world. It was just a pity that Elliot had been forced to go to such lengths. A twinge of regret settled in his stomach, but he resolutely pushed it aside. He'd had no choice in the matter. None at all. Fate hadn't left him any.

And now that his niece had disappeared . . . Elliot scowled. It was yet another delay, and he was tired of delays, tired of waiting for what should have been his all along.

Catherine's disappearance had taken Elliot by surprise. He'd grossly misjudged his niece's determination.

He supposed he shouldn't have—Catherine was more like John than even Royce. She had the same determination, the same unwillingness to bend to life's setbacks. Elliot had discovered that she was missing after she didn't come down to dinner last night. It wasn't an unusual thing for Catherine to go for a long, lonely walk, especially in the days since Royce's disappearance. The girl was mourning her brother and it was only natural that she'd need some time alone.

But dinner had come and gone, the sun lowered well into the horizon before Elliot realized that Catherine hadn't simply gone on a solitary ramble down the beach. He'd sent the servants out to look for her, but to no avail. She was gone and no one had seen her.

Elliot had questioned everyone. At first, he had feared that something unfortunate had happened to her—she'd fallen while climbing the rocks along the beach, or someone had stolen her away . . . but as time passed, he began to realize that Catherine's disappearance had nothing to do with ill chance.

Elliot's gaze rested on the tattered note on the corner of his desk. As unpalatable as it was, he would bet his last coin that his stubborn niece was on her way to Savannah to find her brother.

Not that she'd find anything—Elliot had made sure of

that. It was irritating that he had to take the time to track her down. But his plan was nothing without her. Less than nothing, in fact.

Elliot glanced sourly at the portrait that hung over the fireplace. In it, John and his wife sat on a settee, Catherine in a chair at their side, Royce standing with a hand on each of his parents' shoulders. They looked handsome and wealthy and annoyingly happy. Elliot wrinkled his nose.

He pulled a ledger from the corner of the desk. Fortunately for all concerned, Elliot had the situation under control.

When he'd received the ransom note, he'd immediately seen the opportunity that lay before him. Catherine was easy to control, or so he thought. But Royce . . . that was a different matter altogether. Elliot knew he would have to remove his nephew from the picture. He'd been trying to decide on a course of action when he'd been contacted by a Frenchman named DeGardineau. The man had come to inquire about hiring his ships to the Markham Tea Company.

Within ten minutes, Elliot was certain the scoundrel was a pirate, a liar, a murderer, a cheat, and worse. He was exactly the man Elliot needed. DeGardineau had no fears and even fewer scruples. For the right price, the Frenchman would do whatever asked of him.

Elliot hired DeGardineau on the spot and sent him and his men on their first mission—but not to deliver supplies. Instead they were to find whoever had captured Royce Markham and see to it that the rightful owner of the Markham Tea Company never returned home. DeGardineau had sworn to take care of the matter, and he would, if Catherine did not mess things up with her ill-advised attempt to rescue her brother.

Elliot sighed and reached for a pen and a sheet of paper. He hated the thought, but it appeared that he might need DeGardineau's services one more time. Elliot penned a quick note, sanded it, and neatly sealed it with wax. Then he called for a footman to carry the missive to a certain inn found by the Harbor. DeGardineau would send a man to High Hall before nightfall. He always did.

Feeling better, Elliot opened the ledger and began to check the numbers. DeGardineau's men would stop the *Sea Princess*, and the Markham Tea Company would be his.

CHAPTER SIX

Catherine had to wait a good half hour after Derrick left the cabin before Lucas arrived. He grinned cheekily on seeing her. "There ye are! I've come to take ye to yer cabin."

Catherine stood, George lumbering to his feet beside her. "Of course."

"This way, miss." Lucas set off down the narrow hallway, Catherine in his wake.

They stopped three doors down and waited for George, who was busily sniffing every nook and crevice.

Lucas opened the narrow door and stepped aside. "Here ye are, miss! Ye've the second-best cabin on ship."

Catherine looked at her new quarters dubiously. The room was easily four times smaller than Derrick's. None of the little touches that made Derrick's cabin seem so nice—the red curtains about the bunk, the pillows on the seat by the windows, the brass fixtures on the wall—not a single one was replicated here. The cabin was not only tiny, but it was sparsely furnished, containing only a bunk, one chair, a tiny table decorated with a wash bowl and pitcher, and a rough-hewn trunk. She couldn't help but think of her room at High Hall with the blue curtains and the sun streaming through the large windows.

But this wasn't about comfort and home. It was about Royce. She lifted her chin and managed a smile. "It's just fine."

Lucas beamed. "I'm glad ye like it. 'Tis Smythe's cabin, ye know."

"Smythe's?" Catherine said, taking a step back. "I can't take his cabin!"

"'Course ye can. He'll just bunk elsewhere. He's done it often enough."

Catherine started to argue, but Lucas wouldn't hear a word. He cheerfully asked her if she needed anything else and then without giving her time to answer, he left, pulling the door closed behind him, shutting her and George into their tiny room.

Alone, Catherine sank onto her bunk. George shuffled to her feet and sat, heaving a huge yawn. Then, with a shake of his massive shoulders, he slid into a heap on the floor. Catherine watched, amused, as the dog attempted to get comfortable. He turned this way and that, and finally, with a huge unhappy sigh, folded himself up instead of stretching out like a full-size rug as he normally did. Once he was curled into a ball, he looked up at Catherine with a pained expression.

She laughed and rubbed his ears. "I know exactly what you mean." It was going to take some adjustment for both of them, but whatever they had to bear, it was nothing compared to what Royce must be going through. George sighed happily as she scratched his head. After a moment, still full from the shepherd's pie and tired from her adventures, Catherine followed George's lead. She lay down on the bunk, her fingers still threaded through her dog's thick fur as she thought about the day's events and the coming trip to Savannah.

After thirty minutes passed, someone knocked on the door. Catherine struggled upright, pushing her hair back from her face. Somewhere along the way, she'd lost her ribbon and her shirt had come untucked. She forced the sleep from her mind as she tried to straighten herself. Heavens, but she must look horrible. The knock sounded again.

"Miss Markham?" Smythe's voice was muffled by the thick oak door.

She took two steps, which carried her completely across the small room, and opened the door.

The first mate beamed pleasantly at her. A small bundle wrapped in brown paper and secured with a string rested in his hands. "I've brought ye some clothing like the cap'n ordered."

Catherine took the bundle, almost afraid to open it and see what was inside. "Thank you."

"Ye're welcome, miss. I hope 'tis yer size. I looked fer a green gown to go with yer eyes, but I couldn't find one. Ye don't mind blue, do ye?"

Smythe appeared genuinely worried, and Catherine

grinned. "It's my favorite color."

He beamed. "Why don't ye go ahead and see if the gown fits? Then, if ye're up to it, I'll take ye fer a tour of the ship. If we wait until we're under way, it might be hôurs afore I'm free to take ye."

"Wonderful!" Catherine closed the door and hurried to change. Considering the limited selection vailable, the first mate had chosen the perfect gown. Sky blue with a ruffled trim, it fit her very well, though it was a trifle short. Still, after wearing Royce's cast-off clothing for two days, she was glad to change into something clean and pretty. She even found a comb tucked in the bundle and she took the time to brush out her hair.

Finally feeling more herself, Catherine opened the door.

Smythe was leaning against the opposite wall, his hands jammed into his pockets, his plump stomach overlapping his belt. He straightened when he saw Catherine, his eyes widening. "There now, don't ye look fine!"

She smoothed the skirts of the gown. "It's truly lovely. Thank you, Smythe. For both the gown and the cabin."

"I didn't do nothin' but spend the Cap'n's hard-earned money. Ye'll have to thank him fer that. And as fer the cabin, that don't matter none at all. Lucas don't snore much and whoever bunks with Little gets extra portions of hardtack."

"Well, I still thank you. It was very kind of you."

Smythe grinned amiably. "Shall we go up on deck, miss? We'll be setting sail soon."

She nodded, then allowed Smythe to escort her down the hallway and up the ladder. George followed along, stopping occasionally to sniff an interesting corner.

Earlier, when Catherine had been on deck, she'd had the chance to see a few of the crew members, though many had already gone ashore. The ones who'd been present had paid far more attention to George than to her.

But this time, the second she stepped on deck, something happened. The crew stared. Some began to mutter uneasily, while others cast her glances of such dislike that she was at a loss. Smythe didn't seem to notice, pointing out the various masts and sails, pausing to explain how the ship sailed and what each line was for.

Catherine tried not to notice the reaction of the crew, but it was difficult.

On the other side of the ship a line broke loose and someone shouted. Smythe muttered a curse and then turned bright red. "Sorry about that, miss! It jus' sort of slipped out. Here, you stay with Lucas a moment while I see to that rope."

He nodded to Lucas, who stood a short distance away. The cabin boy came forward quickly and Smythe ordered him to explain things to Miss Markham until he returned. Lucas nodded happily and the first mate scuttled off, barking orders at the sailors closest to the loose line.

"Lucas," Catherine said in a quiet voice. "The crew seems uneasy. Have I done something wrong?"

Lucas shook his head. "Not that I know of, miss."

At just that moment, Catherine caught sight of Derrick. He was standing on the foredeck, his white shirt open at the neck. He was staring at her, an unreadable expression on his face. Looking away from her, he quickly called his crew to order, sending the loudest of the complainers off to do a number of chores.

Catherine looked at her escort. "Lucas, surely something is wrong. Please explain this to me."

He scratched his ear, his face turning as red as his hair. "'Tis the gown, miss."

"The gown? If that's all it is, then I'll change—"

"No, miss. I'm afeared that won't help. The gown bothers 'em cause they didn't know ye was a female afore. They thought ye was a boy."

"What difference does that make?"

"'Tis bad luck to have a woman on board ship. Everyone knows that."

It was fortunate that Catherine didn't believe in superstitions. She wasn't about to let a little thing like the silly beliefs of Derrick's crew make her feel uneasy. Ignoring Lucas's suggestion that they retire from deck, Catherine stayed where she was. Once they got used to her, they wouldn't even know she was there.

But the men couldn't stop looking at her and muttering.

Lines got tangled, sails broke free of their ties, tempers frayed, and heated words were exchanged, almost always ending with someone or another glancing at Catherine.

By the end of the first hour or so, she was certain that the entire crew hated her. But the worst came when Catherine, tired of standing, had moved a bucket so that she could sit on a nearby crate and look out to sea. George had rested at her feet, but after a while, he'd gotten up and wandered off.

Sniffing the air, he shuffled up to the nearest sailor, accidentally bumping the man into another. Catherine hurried off to collect her unruly dog, forgetting about the bucket. Another member of the crew, on his way to relieve the watch, stumbled over the misplaced bucket and slammed headfirst into the mast, knocking himself unconscious.

Catherine rushed to his side. "Oh dear!" She bent over him and winced to see the lump that was appearing on the man's forehead. She glanced over her shoulder and found several crew members gathered around. "I need some cold water!"

"Aye, aye!" one man cried, then hurried off. A moment later he returned holding a bucket. Before Catherine could say a word, he lifted the bucket and tossed the entire contents over the poor man who lay prone on the deck.

The man coughed and sputtered.

"I didn't mean for you to empty it over him!" Catherine

said. "I was just going to put a damp cloth on his head."

"Sorry, miss," the crewman said, setting down the bucket.

Another sailor leaned forward on his toes, trying to see over someone else's shoulder. "Wonder what caused Parsons to fall?"

Everyone looked at the knocked-over bucket. "How did it get out there?" someone said. "'Tis supposed to be tucked against the helm."

Catherine looked at the bucket. Surely that wasn't the bucket she'd moved when she'd tried to find a comfortable seat a few moments ago. Surely she hadn't moved it and then left it.

But she had. "I . . . I think I might have moved it."

Six pairs of eyes fastened on her in accusation. Catherine wished the deck of the ship would open up and drop her into the safety of her small cabin. She cleared her throat. "I—I'm sorry. I should have—"

"Women shouldn't be on ship," one sailor muttered to another.

"And this is proof!" added another, glaring at Catherine.

"I don't know what Cap'n is thinking, but I'm not going to sail on a ship with no woman," someone said loudly.

"Enough!" Derrick's voice cracked like a whip across the deck. "I see six men where there should be only one.

Have you finished your duties so quickly? Perhaps it is time to scrub the decks again."

The sailors turned to go back to their posts, though they muttered as they did so.

Derrick leveled a stern gaze at Catherine. "Go below." His face set in angry lines, he looked anything but sympathetic.

"I was just—"

"Do as I say."

He looked so angry. Catherine started again, "But I was just—"

Derrick slanted her a hard, unyielding look. "If you don't go below, I shall carry you there myself."

Catherine's throat closed up and she realized she was in danger of bursting into tears. She managed a quick nod, and Smythe, who had been hovering nearby, promptly hustled her off the deck, muttering soothing words like "let the Cap'n handle everything" and how "a nice li'l nap" would do her wonders.

He took her to her cabin and, after pointing out the fresh pitcher of water on the side table, he'd hovered until she'd sent him away. As soon as Smythe left, Catherine pulled off the gown, tossed it into a corner with far more force than necessary, and jammed her legs back into Royce's cast-off breeches, vowing to never wear another dress again.

But it was no good. Even as she was buttoning Royce's shirt, her lagging spirits collapsed and she dropped onto her bunk, buried her face in her pillow, and cried. All of her life she'd known who and what she was—Catherine Markham of High Hall. And that had been enough. But now, with Royce missing, Catherine had begun to realize how important her family was. Royce especially.

She had to find him. She had to.

George rested his nose against her shoulder, offering what comfort he could. After a long cry, Catherine finally fell into a deep, dreamless sleep.

It was much later when she finally awoke, her cabin dark except for a lantern that had been hung on a peg by the door. The soft glow lit up the plate of food that sat on the table. Whoever had brought her the lamp and food had also picked up her dress and hung it neatly over a chair. Catherine blinked the sleep from her eyes and pushed her hair from her face, noticing that the ship seemed to be heeling slightly to one side. They'd set sail. Catherine sighed her satisfaction.

She stretched, made her way to the table, and lifted the plate's cover. A feeling of well-being filtered through her as she ate the mutton stew. Though it was no longer warm, it was still quite tasty.

She quickly finished the meal and placed the remains on the floor for George, who promptly wolfed it down and then lay licking every inch of the plate.

Catherine returned to the bunk, where she lay thinking of what Royce must be doing now. She hoped he was not hungry or cold. . . . It was a relief to know that it was May and the wind not as chilled.

Restless, Catherine sat up and swung her feet to the floor. She'd deliver the ransom money herself, no matter what it took. "Regardless of Derrick St. John, blast him," she muttered. The cabin suddenly seemed dark and dreary. Catherine rose and rinsed her face in the basin of water on the small washstand, noting that even the bowl was attached to the stand. Then, patting George and telling him to behave, she smoothed her hair and headed for the deck.

Catherine paused on the last step of the ladder and looked up at the evening sky. A brisk wind washed the silvered deck, tugging her hair and riffling her shirt. Stars shone and a lantern cast mysterious shadows across the night sea. Catherine looked about her cautiously and was glad to see that most of the crew was below deck.

In fact, she saw only two men, and one of them was Lucas, who nodded when he saw her.

Catherine smiled back, relaxing a little as she made her way to the railing across the deck. The wind filled the sails, swelling them into billowing night clouds overhead. She stopped to admire the proud stance of the mainmast when the deck suddenly lifted high on the crest of a wave, then slashed downward.

Catherine barely managed to stay upright, stumbling back into a wall. She clutched at it, frowning when her fingers clamped onto cloth. The ship steadied and

Catherine peered upward. She stood against the hard wall of Derrick's chest, her fingers clutched about his shirt.

"Sorry," she muttered, stepping backward.

His hands came to rest on her shoulders and he left them there, his fingers warm. "Steady there. What are you doing up here?"

Catherine thought she detected a critical note in his voice and she jutted out her chin. "I was taking a walk. It's a free ship, isn't it?"

His smile glinted in the moonlight, the wind tossing his dark hair. "Yes, but only if you don't wreak havoc with my men."

"I didn't do anything but move a bucket. I certainly didn't know that man was going to walk where the bucket was and—"

"Easy, Catherine. I know." His hands slid down her arms to capture her hands, he gave them a gentle squeeze before he released them. "I didn't mean to be so abrupt with you before, but I needed time to talk to the crew."

Catherine looked down at her hands. His skin had been rough and warm against hers. "Did you speak to the men?"

"Yes."

"Then . . . they no longer think I'm bad luck?"

"It's not so much that women are bad luck as it is that they are distracting. And you were quite distracting in that blue dress."

Somewhere in there was a compliment of sorts.

Catherine blinked up at Derrick. "Did *you* think I was distracting?"

"Such a distraction on a ship can cause accidents," Derrick explained, ignoring her question, "which is how the superstition arose to begin with."

"I wasn't trying to cause any problems."

"I know. I hope you don't mind, but I had to reveal the reason you are on board. I think they'll be more cooperative now."

"I hope so." She managed a faint smile. "I don't think George can handle any more days like today."

"George, eh?" Derrick's gaze ran across her, warm and almost . . . possessive, somehow. "I wasn't worried about that mutt. I was worried about you. Where is he, anyway?"

"I left him in my cabin."

"Good for you." He smiled, and for an instant she caught a glimpse of a different, lighthearted Derrick. She bit her lip and looked away. He confused her; one moment he was abrupt and cold, and the next he was smiling down at her intimately.

Catherine stepped away from Derrick, shivering a little in the cold. "There's no reason to worry about me or George. I can handle us both."

Derrick turned toward the railing, his face hidden in the shadows, his hair glinting blue black. "So you say."

Catherine glanced at him through her lashes. Though the ship rolled with the waves, he stood with his feet planted firmly, his white shirt open at the throat, the wide sleeves of his coat turned back to reveal his strong arms. The wind rippled through his hair as he lifted his face toward the breeze.

He looked older than his twenty-one years, the burden of responsibility resting firmly on his shoulders. Even if she hadn't known it, she would have been able to tell that he was in command of the ship and the hardened men who crewed her.

For one instant, Catherine was glad events had conspired to put her in Derrick's way somewhere other than High Hall, where he hardly spoke to her. And why was that? she suddenly wondered. She had avoided him, of course, but that was only because he made her feel like she was a nuisance. Normally, Catherine hadn't cared about such things . . . but Derrick had always made her feel self-conscious.

His gaze went to the sky. "You can see more stars at sea than anywhere else."

She followed his gaze. The velvet black sky was thick with glistening stars. They touched the invisible horizon and rose high above her head. "It's beautiful."

He glanced at her and nodded. "I love the sea. I always have."

Catherine wondered what exactly had happened to make Derrick so driven. She tried to remember the few details she knew of Derrick's past. His father had been captain of a ship called the *Valiant*. Catherine remembered the name because she'd thought at the time that it was a fitting name for a traitor's ship. And a traitor was what people called Derrick's father.

It was rumored that the *Valiant* had joined the British for an undisclosed sum of money, hiring out like a pirate vessel. With a sack of British gold resting in her hold, the ship had attacked an American frigate. The frigate had returned fire, but was badly outmanned by the lighter, more elusive ship and Captain St. John's superior knowledge of military strategy.

The frigate would have fallen had it not been for a French ship that had caught sight of the smoke from the cannon and come to its aid. Once the French joined the fray, the battle swung against the *Valiant*. Catherine wasn't sure what happened then, but Captain St. John would never see another day—he perished during the battle and only his crew lived to tell the tale.

Royce hadn't believed it, of course. He'd declared that the truth would come out at the inquest. Instead, crew member after crew member stepped forward to swear that Captain St. John had indeed taken money from the British and then forced the crew to attack the American ship. The judge had ruled that the evidence proved that Captain St. John was guilty of attacking a ship from his own country—and it had branded him a traitor.

Royce had told Catherine that Derrick felt responsible for the black mark against his father's name. He thought it was made more believable by his own terrible reputation for piracy.

She felt Derrick shift beside her, his arm brushing hers. It was cooler now, the salty wind spraying a mist over her. She closed her eyes and lifted her face to the coolness. On board the ship, Derrick seemed so much older, so self-contained and serious. He was a full-grown man, one with responsibilities far beyond his age. It made her feel younger than her seventeen years.

Nonsense, she told herself. She turned, resting her back against the railing so that she could look up at his stern profile. *He is no different from Royce, just as irritating, bossy, and too full of his own worth to realize—*

"Do you always talk to yourself?"

Startled, Catherine blinked. "Was I talking just now?" She hoped not. If he had heard what she was thinking—

He grinned widely, his eyes crinkling at the corners. "Not this time, but I've heard you do it several times. You also talk in your sleep."

"How do you know I—" She remembered waking and finding the mutton stew in her cabin. "You brought my dinner."

"And a lamp." Derrick leaned against the railing beside her, his hip warm against hers. "You were having a fine discussion with yourself."

Catherine desperately tried to remember what she'd dreamed, but all she could remember was a strange muddle of sights and sounds, most of them having to do with Royce. "I only talk to myself when there are no acceptable humans about."

"I'm acceptable. You can talk to me." He smiled down at her.

The ship chose that moment to list to one side and Catherine stumbled sharply. Derrick caught her before she fell and steadied her against him.

She looked up into his smoke blue eyes, her breath caught in her throat. Heavens, he was tall. She pulled away and he immediately released her. "Thank you. I'm not used to the sway of the ship," she said, shivering a little.

His gaze flickered across her face to her mouth. "You're cold," he said, noticing her shiver. He slipped off his coat and put it about her shoulders, his hands brushing against her neck as he did so.

Something happened then—the air thickened, the sights and sounds about them melted away and all Catherine knew was that she was standing with Derrick, their bodies separated only by the thickness of their clothes. Her stomach tightened and she felt as if she'd never breathe again.

His mouth lowered toward hers, hovering a breath away.

"Derrick," she whispered, closing her eyes and waiting.

But as suddenly as he'd caught her, Derrick stepped

back, his movement so abrupt that she staggered back against the railing. For a moment, neither said a word, but stood facing each other, neither seeming to breath.

"Catherine, I—" Derrick rubbed a hand over his face. "I didn't mean to do that."

It was bad enough that he had stepped away, but to apologize as if he'd done something wrong . . . She leaned forward and rested her forehead against his chest, refusing to look at him. The coat smelled of salt and wind and the ocean. And of Derrick. She took a deep breath, inhaling the scent.

She didn't know what had just happened; maybe he'd suddenly realized how young she was. How she was nothing like the women he normally spoke to. They were probably older, and more experienced, and probably far more interesting.

For the first time in her life, Catherine realized how little she'd actually experienced. Her life at High Hall had seemed full and busy, but beside Derrick's life, her own seemed pale and unexciting.

Derrick covered her hands with his and gently moved her away. "Catherine, please don't look like that. I'm sorry, I shouldn't have tried— It will never happen again. You have my word."

His word that he'd never try to kiss her again? For some reason that made her feel worse than his apology. Catherine had to swallow twice before she could answer.

"It was nothing," she said as lightly as she could. "I—I think I should go below."

Derrick looked as if he might say something more, but his words were interrupted by the sound of heavy footsteps scrambling for purchase on the short ladder. Huffing and puffing followed before Smythe appeared.

"Lord love ye, Cap'n, but the ladder seems to be gettin' longer every day."

Derrick didn't look very happy at the interruption, but he managed a brief smile. "'Tis your girth that is growing, Symthe. Not the ladder."

The first mate patted his stomach fondly. "That may be, Cap'n, but 'tis a good paunch as protects me from the cold. When we get a bit farther north, ye'll be wishin' ye had some o' this yerself." He suddenly looked from Derrick to Catherine. "Did I interrupt ye? I could go back below fer a while if ye think ye—"

"No," Catherine said quickly. "Of course not. Der—I mean, the captain was just explaining to me why the crew thinks I'm bad luck."

"Weel now, that was right unmannerly o' him, wasn't it?" Smythe shot a sharp glance at Derrick, but then he sighed. "Unfortunately, 'tis also true. The men can't think when there's a woman about. It makes 'em a mite restive."

"So they blame the women? That doesn't seem fair."

Symthe rubbed a finger across his nose as if it itched very badly. "Who would we blame, then?"

"Why, the men, of course," Catherine said, amazed she had to even explain the logic.

Smythe seemed to consider this, for he rocked back on his heels and pursed his lips. But after a moment he shook his head. "But no one would be actin' like anythin' if a woman wasn't on ship. And so 'tis obviously the woman at fault."

Catherine opened her mouth to argue when Derrick broke in, "I believe it's getting cold. I'll see you to your cabin."

"Yes, but I want to tell Smythe—"

Derrick captured her arm and led her toward the ladder, his fingers gripping her elbow through the thick coat. "I'm sure it will wait until tomorrow." He raised his voice, "Won't it, Smythe?"

"Aye, Cap'n," the first mate returned with a cheerful wave of his hand. "I'll find Miss Markham at first light."

Hand clasped about her wrist, Derrick led her down the narrow hall to her cabin. When they arrived, he opened the door, then stood aside.

Catherine started to enter her room, her mind whirling with all the things she felt she should say but couldn't find the words for. Suddenly she stopped. "Your coat." She slipped it off her shoulders and held it out to him.

He took the coat and stepped back. "Good night, Catherine." His voice was low and deep, almost husky in the quiet of the ship.

"Good night," she answered in return, wanting something more, but not sure what.

He nodded once, then turned and left, his footsteps quickly receding. Catherine remained in the doorway of her cabin, her gaze glued to the spot where Derrick had just been.

He was an honorable man. He would never kiss a woman who did not wish him to. But that was the problem; Catherine *wanted* to be kissed. She suddenly realized she *wanted* to feel his lips on hers. The thought shocked Catherine.

George nudged her hand, his cold nose wet against her palm. She immediately bent and hugged him, pressing her cheek to the dog's furry head. "But he doesn't see me as someone to be kissed."

George wagged his tail and Catherine hugged him the harder. "He sees me as his best friend's little sister and nothing more." She sighed, her breath stirring the fur on George's head. "I just wish he—"

No, she wouldn't finish that thought. Not tonight. Perhaps not ever. "That's fine," she told George, taking his head between her hands and looking into his brown eyes. "I don't need Derrick St. John to kiss me. Once Royce is safe, you and I will travel the world. I'll become the most sophisticated, entrancing girl Derrick St. John has ever seen. He'll be sorry he didn't kiss me then."

George panted his approval, wagging his tail so hard it

thumped the wood floor like a drum. Catherine chuckled and hugged him. That's exactly what she'd do once they saved Royce. All she had to do now was stay away from Derrick St. John so that she didn't make a fool of herself.

Fortunately, Savannah was only a week away. But never had a week seemed so long. Sighing, Catherine closed the door to her cabin and prepared for bed.

❧

CHAPTER SEVEN

Catherine spent the next two days avoiding Derrick. Overall, she was very successful, though it was difficult since they were on a ship, even one as large as the *Sea Princess*.

Though she managed not to be alone with him, she couldn't completely remove him from her thoughts. It was strange, but the more time she spent with him, the less she was able to control her own feelings. And Catherine was beginning to believe she was capable of having very strong feelings indeed.

For his part, Derrick seemed not to mind, which she found particularly annoying. He made absolutely no effort to speak to her, though he watched her constantly, his blue gaze following her whenever he chanced to see her. She tried to take some comfort in that small fact and resolved to have nothing more to do with him.

Not that it was easy. He was so attractive, with that black hair falling over his forehead and those intense blue eyes. Catherine was hard-pressed not to linger in his vicinity whenever he was on deck.

Fortunately, lovable, furry George came to her rescue.

Someone began whispering that whoever rubbed the dog's ears would have good luck. Catherine rather suspected Smythe had started the rumor in an effort to gain George some acceptance among the crew, though she couldn't prove it. Still, it worked; the entire crew lined up to pat the huge mongrel whenever Catherine took him for a walk.

George was in heaven. For Catherine, the contact with the crew allowed her to exchange a few words. In turn, they seemed more at ease with her presence on board.

For two entire, glorious days, Catherine wandered the deck, the wind against her face, her hair flying wildly. Despite her mixed emotions about the ship's captain, she felt free and unrestrained, especially wearing breeches and the loose white shirt, with George lumbering behind her. One of Catherine's favorite crew members, other than Smythe and Lucas, was Tom Poole, the bos'n's mate. It was his job to inspect the sails and rigging every morning and report their condition to the officer on watch.

Tom was older than most of the other sailors, his eyes lined by past smiles, his long, gray hair neatly tied back with a black leather string. He taught Catherine the names of every line of rigging that strung up the sails. She learned that the *Sea Princess* was square-rigged, that is, she had three masts and was as lightweight a ship as danced upon the water. At first Catherine didn't understand why being lighter was such a good thing, until Tom explained that it meant that the ship could navigate shallower water and escape many of her larger, more cumbersome enemies.

Catherine tilted her head back and stared up at the yards of billowing canvas overhead. "There may only be three masts, but there must be fifty sails."

Tom grinned, a gaping hole where his front teeth should have been. "Aye, miss. There's a number of sails, though not fifty."

"What's that sail at the very top?"

Tom tilted his head back and shaded his eyes. "The royal. Just below her is the topgallant. And the lowermost is the topsail. If ye want a closer look, I'm certain Lucas would climb with ye a bit. I'd take ye meself, but . . ." Tom rubbed his left leg and grimaced.

"Did you fall from the masts?"

"Lord love ye, miss! O' course I didn't fall from the masts." He appeared injured that she'd even suggested such a thing.

"Oh. Then . . . did you hurt yourself in a sea battle?"

"Ah!" Tom wrinkled his nose thoughtfully. "Ye might say that, miss. I came home from sea and me precious li'l Meggie threw a heavy pot at me head 'cause I didn't think to bring her all me pay." He sighed soulfully. "The wench missed me head, but she got me knee straight on."

"I see," Catherine said. "Meggie must be a very strict wife."

Tom blinked. "Wife? Meggie's no wife. She's a doxy—"

"Poole!"

Catherine turned to find Derrick standing on the fore-castle, frowning down at Tom.

The bos'n's mate straightened his shoulders. "Aye, Cap'n?"

"I don't believe Miss Markham needs to hear about Meggie's lifestyle."

Tom blinked, a red patch slowly coloring his neck and face. He shot a self-conscious look at Catherine. "I didn't think—I should—I needs to . . ." He gulped. "I'd best get on with me duties."

"An excellent idea," Derrick said.

Catherine watched the bos'n's mate scurry off before she cast an irritated glance at Derrick. "Why did you do that? We were just talking."

"You didn't need to hear about Tom's Meggie. In fact, *none* of us need to hear about Tom's Meggie."

She frowned, wishing Derrick wasn't standing above her so that she had to crane her neck to see him. "I don't need protecting."

"Don't you?" He leaned his elbows on the railing and smiled down at her, the wind whipping his dark hair. "What *do* you need, Catherine Markham?"

"Passage to Savannah and nothing more."

"I'll get you to Savannah; you have my word." He considered her for a moment. "What were you and Tom discussing?"

"Before he mentioned Meggie? The ship's rigging."

"You are in luck. I can tell you all about the rigging. In fact, I can teach you everything you need to know."

Catherine's heart leaped at the thought and it was with a bit of regret that she said, "That won't be necessary." She was already far too intrigued with Derrick St. John—spending a breezy afternoon strolling the deck with him would only increase her fascination for him. "But thank you for your offer—it was most kind. I think."

He raised his brows. "What do you mean by that?"

She eyed him for a moment. "You haven't said a nice word to me in two days. Why are you being nice all of a sudden?"

"I'm always nice!"

Catherine just looked at him.

He gave a rueful smile. "Most of the time. Look, I'm sorry. This situation is difficult for both of us. I suppose I just realized that you and I are on the same side and perhaps it's time we acted like it."

She couldn't help smiling in return, and all of her resolution not to speak to him went sailing away on the brisk breeze. "It would make it easier if we did attempt to get along."

"Infinitely. And since I deprived you of Mr. Poole's expert information, the least I can do is make up for it." Derrick placed his hands on the railing and leaped easily across, landing directly before her.

Catherine took a startled step backward. This was not

at all what she'd planned. "Derrick, I really don't—"

"What do you want to know?"

She blinked. What did she want to know? She wanted to know what it was like to live on the ocean. To experience the wild force of a storm. To capture a pirate ship. She wanted to know what it was like to live for the moment— and what it was like to be kissed by Derrick St. John.

Unable to meet his clear gaze, she looked out at the ocean. "I want to know why you love sailing."

"I thought you wanted to know about the ship, not me."

"I want to know about both." She turned to face him. "Why *do* you love sailing?"

He crossed his arms over his chest, tilting his head to one side as his blue gaze fastened on her. "How do you know I love it? Perhaps I find being at sea only passable, a way to make a living."

"I can tell you love it because you're different when you're on your ship."

"How so?"

"You're more certain of yourself." She pursed her lips and thought a moment. "And bossier."

He gave her a lopsided grin that made her heart hum. "Bossier, eh? That's strange, coming from you."

She plopped her hands on her hips. "Are you saying that *I'm* bossy?"

"You said *I* was," he pointed out fairly.

"Yes, well, I merely pointed it out because you are."

He flashed her a rare smile as a gust of wind fluttered the folds of his shirt over his broad shoulders and chest. "I have to command this ship, Catherine. I am supposed to be bossy. Meanwhile you . . ." He shrugged.

"I have to command, too. I've been in charge of High Hall since my mother died when I was thirteen. Royce took over the business, but I took over the house."

His grin widened. "Now you sound like my mother."

"Where is your mother? Does she ever come with you?"

"No, she stays at home and tends to the house and the farm. I see her every chance I get. She's . . ." His smile faded, replaced with a wistful sadness. "She's a wonderful mother. Always has been." He leaned against the railing and looked out to sea. "I just never realized how much until . . ."

"Until what?"

"Until I was older. She's a lot like you, Catherine. She has a lot of responsibilities running the place by herself without my father, but she never complains."

"I didn't say I never complained," Catherine said with a swift smile. "But I wouldn't have it any other way. High Hall is my home. There are more than thirty servants and I have to make sure they complete their duties." It was an immense responsibility, and one that she had struggled with for months and months after her mother's death.

It had taken Catherine almost a year before she felt

comfortable with her role. Now, of course, she didn't even think about it.

Derrick's gaze darkened. "I never thought of that."

"You should have. It's not unlike captaining a ship."

"You are right," he said, eyeing her with new respect. After a moment, he said, "You're different here, on board ship."

"How?"

"You talk more, for one thing. You never said more than two words to me in all the times I visited Royce at High Hall."

"That's because I didn't think you'd want to talk to me," Catherine confided. "You are older than I, and I thought you'd think I was just bothering you."

His smile faded. "You cannot have thought that."

"I did." The wind whipped across them, blowing Catherine's hair across her face. She noticed that the clouds were darker than before. "I'm not the only one who was silent. You rarely spoke to me either."

"That's different. I am not a fit person for you to know."

"Not a . . ." She blinked. "What a ridiculous thing to say!"

Derrick gave her a bitter smile. "There is a reason I'm never invited to the parties and events held by your friends and the other wealthy families in Boston."

She frowned up at him. "It isn't because of your father, is it? I think that's horridly unfair."

His mouth tightened. "No," he said shortly. "It isn't because of my father."

Despite his tone, he looked so lost that she felt she had to say something. "As soon as we return, I'm going to see to it that you are invited to all of the parties and events. Wait and see."

"No. You don't want your name tangled with mine."

Catherine lifted her chin. "That's my decision, isn't it? I wouldn't be a good person if I didn't point out to my friends when they have made an error."

He chuckled at that. "When you lift your chin like that, you look exactly like Royce."

"He believes in you," Catherine persisted. "I don't know how many times I've heard him say that he thinks you are the most honorable man he knows."

Derrick's face hardened and he looked away. After a moment, he said in a strained voice. "I owe your brother everything."

"You've paid him back a hundredfold. He told me you were his most profitable captain. That's worth a lot."

"I could never repay him for trusting me when no one else would." He straightened suddenly. "Come. I'm about to have the crew adjust course. You can watch from the foredeck."

Though Catherine wasn't finished with their conversation, Derrick clearly was. So she followed him up the ladder and spent the next hour watching the crew untie and retie a hundred different knots as they moved the sails. But even as she watched the men, Catherine was aware of Derrick by her side.

The next day dawned blustery and gray, the sails billowing wildly. There was an air of expectancy among the men. Catherine felt it the moment she stepped on deck.

Smythe hurried by.

"Is something wrong?" Catherine managed to ask as he trotted past.

He didn't stop. "Storm brewing. We're trying to lash everything in place afore she hits."

Catherine followed him, lengthening her stride until she was almost running to keep up with him. "Will the ship survive a storm?"

"She's light, but we'll hug the shoreline." Smythe glanced over his shoulder. "Perhaps ye'd best go below, miss. 'Tis not safe on deck if that storm is as strong as Cap'n thinks it is." He stopped long enough to give her a quick wink and then he was gone, barking orders and urging the men to hurry.

Catherine looked up at the sky. It looked as it had the day before, the clouds racing overhead. But there was a different feel to the wind, an excitement that hadn't been there before.

She caught sight of Derrick on the foredeck. He stood, calmly giving orders though the wind pushed and pulled with an unusual strength.

Catherine walked toward him. She was just passing the mizzenmast when a yell came from the crow's nest. "Ship ho!"

She stopped and glanced out to sea. A faint outline danced on the horizon.

Derrick whipped out his spyglass and stared out to sea. The wind plastered his shirt across his chest and flat stomach. Not that Catherine noticed, of course. She was immune to him now. He was like any other dashing, daring sea captain she knew.

Derrick lowered the glass. From where Catherine stood she couldn't make out his voice, but she thought he cursed. Unconsciously, she began to walk a bit faster toward the deck, straining to hear.

"What is it, Cap'n?" Smythe asked, clambering up the steps to reach Derrick's side. Catherine ambled up the steps after him, her curiosity getting the better of her.

Derrick glanced at her briefly, a frown between his eyes. But to Catherine's surprise, he didn't order her below. Instead, he turned to Smythe. "'Tis a ship. Coming from the east."

The first mate appeared concerned. "East? Can you make out her flag?"

"Aye," Derrick spat out. "She's flying a Jolly Roger."

"Pirates!" Smythe exclaimed. "But . . . they can't be after us. We haven't picked up our shipment yet and we've no haul."

Catherine turned to find Lucas at her elbow, his eyes wide. "How could the pirates know what we are carrying?"

"'Cause we're ridin' so high in the water," Lucas answered. "'Course, we could be carryin' something of value that didn't weigh so much as cotton or tea, but 'tis unlikely."

Catherine nodded, turning her attention back to Derrick.

"They're coming this way," he said. He snapped the glass closed and returned it to a pouch at his waist. "We're going to have to make a run for it. Ready the ship, Smythe."

"Aye, Cap'n." The pudgy first mate leaned over the railing and yelled, "Man the deck! Prepare fer attack! We've guests, lads, so step lively!"

His words sent a wild flurry of activity across the ship. Men poured out of every opening and swarmed the deck. Sails were adjusted, barrels relashed, and kegs of shot and powder were hauled to the outer railing. Before Catherine's bemused gaze, sixteen cannon were unlashed from their moorings and pushed to one side of the ship, where they were neatly tied in place.

Derrick seemed curiously calm, his sharp gaze watching every movement of his men even as he checked the progress of the approaching ship.

"She's a large 'un, Cap'n," Smythe said as the ship moved closer. "She'll have thirty-two–pound shot, if not more."

"We could probably outrun her. It's a damnable shame the wind's against us." Derrick pulled the spyglass out one more time and examined the approaching ship.

Catherine stepped back into a corner as men bustled by. Surely they weren't going to really engage in battle. It was probably a mistake, she told herself, her heart pounding in her chest. She couldn't look away from the other ship. It hung on the horizon, dark and menacing, inching ever closer.

Catherine realized that the men had ceased preparing. They were at their stations, all eyes focused on the approaching danger.

From behind her, Derrick said, "Miss Markham, go below."

Catherine looked around and met Derrick's blue gaze. "I want to stay here." The thought of sitting alone in her cabin while Derrick and his men risked their lives was too frightening to contemplate.

His jaw tightened. "You shall go below. *Now.*"

Catherine closed her lips over her protest. As much as

she'd like to, it was not the time to engage in an argument. She gave an abrupt nod and turned toward the ladder.

Behind her, Smythe cursed.

Catherine halted, one foot still on the top step of the ladder.

Derrick's mouth appeared almost white with tension. "Bring the *Sea Princess* about."

"Cap'n?"

"Do it, Smythe. If we run into that storm we'll be in even more danger than we are now."

The first mate sighed, then nodded, yelling an indecipherable string of orders that sent the silent men tumbling to work.

Catherine felt as if she were in a bad dream. The pirate ship was close enough now that she could see the details of the ship, even trace the lines of the rigging.

Her heart in her throat, Catherine watched six men ready a cannon, pouring in powder and a small cannonball, and then tamping it all in with a large ramrod.

"Turn her starboard, Smythe," Derrick said.

Smythe frowned. "Starboard, Cap'n? But that'll have us sailing directly toward—"

"I know what starboard is," Derrick snapped. "Do as ordered."

"Aye, Cap'n," Smythe said unhappily. He passed the order on, then turned to look at the approaching ship.

Good heavens, but they were turning . . . sailing *toward* the pirate ship. The men muttered uneasily, but Derrick remained still as stone, his gaze on the approaching ship.

The two ships danced closer and closer, the waves cresting in menacing white caps, the sky hanging lower. Suddenly, a deep boom sounded from across the sea and Catherine held her breath. A cannonball passed directly overhead, crashing through one of the sails and then on into the ocean beyond.

"Return fire, Cap'n?" Smythe asked.

"No," Derrick said, his face set in grim lines. "Not yet."

Another cannonball raced toward them, though this one fell short, plopping harmlessly into the sea.

"Now, Cap'n?" Smythe asked again, his face damp with sweat.

"Not yet. She's barely in range and I won't waste our shot."

Boom! A cannonball whistled through the air, seeming to head directly at them. This one hit the side of the foredeck with a thundering *crack* that made the entire ship rock. Catherine stumbled against a barrel, her hip thudding on the iron band around the top. She grasped the barrel and held on, closing her eyes and trying to catch her breath. Through the noise and confusion, she could hear Derrick's voice.

"Damage, Smythe?"

"We were lucky, Cap'n. It made a clean hole into the mess hall. No one was about."

"Good. Full speed ahead."

"But Cap'n . . . shouldn't we at least try and make a run fer it? I don't mean to question yer orders, but—"

"Do as I say."

Another shot was fired, and this time the ball hit the center of the main deck.

Someone screamed and wood splintered. The noise was deafening and Catherine closed her eyes, praying as she had never prayed before. Over it all, she heard Derrick's deep voice booming out orders. Someone screamed "Man down!" and Catherine watched as two men picked up a limp body and carried it to one side.

"It's Lucas," Smythe said, his voice shrill.

"How badly is he wounded?"

"I don't know. A bit of the railing slammed into his chest." Smythe shook his head. "It looks bad, Cap'n."

Derrick's mouth went white, but he didn't move his eyes from the enemy ship.

"Cap'n?" Smythe asked, his voice shrill. "Should we trim the sail? 'Tis madness to run straight at them. Ye . . . ye don't mean to ram them, do ye?"

"Full sail, Smythe."

Smythe swallowed hard, clearly unhappy. But all he said was, "Aye, aye, Cap'n."

Smythe might be under Derrick's spell, but Catherine

was not. She wanted to protest. They were flying toward danger, not away from it.

Another boom sounded, then another. Soon a volley of cannon came their way. Most shots went awry, several came close to hitting the mainmast. Two of them ripped through the sails. One whistled close by and Catherine could see that it was going to hit the deck. Men scrambled to get out of the way.

It hit with a huge *crack* that rocked the entire ship. Wood splintered and smoke poured forth.

"Put out that fire!" Derrick yelled.

"Cap'n!" Smythe said, his pudgy face pale. "We're in their firing range! We've got to turn—"

"Hold to course!" Derrick snapped.

Smythe gulped, but nodded.

The ships moved closer and the cannon fire continued. Several other shots came close to deck, but many went wide. Smoke drifted across the deck and the men muttered uneasily.

Catherine peeked through the railing at the attacking ship. It was a beautiful thing, the two ships dancing in the waves, coming closer and closer. Beautiful and deadly. Catherine shivered and watched as two more cannonballs thundered toward them. One hit the mainsail and ripped a huge hole in it, while the other passed harmlessly over the ship and crashed into the water on the other side.

"Cap'n, should I tell the men to return fire?" Smythe said.

Derrick stood, hands clasped behind his back, the wind whipping through his dark hair, his eyes as cold as ash. Another cannon was fired from the pirate ship, passing over the *Sea Princess* and harmlessly splashing into the ocean on the other side.

A faint smile touched Derrick's mouth. Catherine rubbed her hip and wondered what he thought was so humorous. The men muttered and cursed, but they all stayed at their posts. Catherine realized that it was a testament to how much they trusted their captain. They might not understand his intentions, but they were willing to let him decide their fate.

The sea roiled and pitched as the wind picked up, the storm heavy above them, the clouds as menacing as the ship that plowed their way. Smoke and fire belched from the pirate ship's cannon as another shot lobbed overhead, then splashed into the sea on the other side of the ship. Another followed suit.

Derrick's face suddenly broke into a grin. "We're under their range," he said, and Catherine heard the relief in his voice. "Smythe, fire when ready."

"Under their . . ." Smythe blinked, then gave a shout of laughter. "We're under their range, mates!" He leaned over the railing. "Fire when ready!"

That was all it took. The cannon burst into action,

belching smoke and fire. The acrid scent of sulfur burned Catherine's nose. She glanced at Smythe, who stood grinning from ear to ear.

"He waited until you were close enough to do some damage," Catherine yelled over the cannon fire.

Smythe nodded, grinning. "Large ships use thirty-two–pound shot. It can cause some goodly damage, but it takes a heavy cannon to fire it and they cannot shorten their range. Nor can they aim as well from such a distance. Once we got our ship inside their firing range . . . well now, 'tis a more even fight."

"What kind of cannon does the *Sea Princess* have?"

"Six-pound shot. Can't cause so much harm, but we can sting a mite." Smythe grinned. "And at this range, we'll not miss a shot."

It was true. Every shot from the *Sea Princess* rendered some damage. They hit the pirate's cannon, the mainmast, and blew holes in the deck.

The *Sea Princess* lurched. "The wind's shiftin'!" Smythe called, his smile fading.

Derrick cursed. "Bring her about! I daresay our friends over there have had enough."

Smythe gave the order and soon the *Sea Princess* was limping away. Derrick leaned over the rail to check on Lucas's condition while Smythe looked up at the torn sails overhead. "We'll have a racking time mending those sails."

"But it can be done?" Catherine asked.

"Of course. We've plenty of canvas to make patchin'
and—" Smythe frowned as he caught sight of some
movement on the deck of the pirate ship. "Cap'n! She's
tacking!"

"What?" Derrick whirled from the railing. "That
doesn't make any sense. We're not loaded and we've
nothing of value on board."

"They think we do," Smythe said grimly.

Derrick nodded. "We've no choice. Ready the men."

Smythe insured the new directions. Derrick caught
sight of Catherine and his brows lowered. "Get below!"

She immediately turned to climb down the ladder,
suddenly all too willing to find the comfort of her bunk.
But as she went, the wind shifted, the ship lurched and a
wave of freezing water crashed across the deck. Catherine
lost her grip. She fell to one side, landing on the deck with
a thud. Cold water swept over her and for a moment, she
slid across the slick wooden surface toward the edge.

Something scooped her from the deck just as she
gasped a cry for help. Strong arms clutched her to a broad
chest and she tried to breath. She opened her eyes and
found herself staring in Derrick's concerned face. "Cap'n!"
Smythe called. "They've all hands on deck and I can see
grappling hooks. They're going to board us."

Derrick cursed and looked down at Catherine. "Are
you all right?"

"I think so," she said shakily. She struggled to stand,

but pain shot up her leg. Derrick didn't say a word, but scooped her back into his arms. All around them, the crew was running into place, knives and guns at the ready. A haze of smoke covered the deck and lent an unreal feeling to the moment.

"I—I'm fine," Catherine managed, though she didn't know if she could put her weight on her ankle.

"No, you're not fine," Derrick said. He carried her to a stack of barrels that were lashed to the deck. He set her down behind the largest one. "Get behind these and hide. No matter what happens, do not come out until I come for you."

Catherine was too confused to answer. She was cold and frightened and thoroughly befuddled.

He tilted her face to his. "Do you understand?"

She met his gaze, and she was suddenly afraid for him—she was safely hidden, but he would be standing on the foredeck, in full sight of the enemy. The thought terrified her, and all she could do was nod.

He hesitated, then bent and brushed a rough kiss across her mouth. His lips were firm and warm and she leaned toward him. It ended all too quickly. "I'll come for you. Hide here until I do."

Catherine pressed her fingers to her lips, her mind whirling to a halt. He had kissed her. The sounds of battle faded and all she could think, see, hear was Derrick. Why had he kissed her? Was it possible he cared for her?

She couldn't make her lips move to ask the question. She just stared at him, her emotions in a turmoil, her body frozen in place.

Smythe yelled something unintelligible and Derrick turned, then hesitated. He pulled his gun from where he'd had it tucked in his waistband and handed it to her. "If they manage to board us, make your way below deck and lock yourself in my cabin. According to the rules of war, they cannot take women prisoner, but these are pirates and I'll not take any chances."

She nodded, the gun cold in her hands. Derrick must have realized her confusion, for he smiled briefly and smoothed back a strand of her hair that was blowing across her face. "Easy, Catherine. We'll make it. See if we don't."

Catherine managed a smile, and then he was gone, heading back to the foredeck with wide, purposeful strides, snapping orders at everyone he saw. He slowed as he passed by Lucas, who was being carried from deck, his shirt soaked with blood.

The sight filled Catherine's eyes with tears. Lucas had been her friend since she arrived at the *Sea Princess*. She struggled to her feet. "Bring him here," she told the men. "I'll tend him."

The men looked at Derrick and he nodded. "Let her do as she says. We've not much time."

Catherine followed Derrick's gaze and gasped. The

pirate ship was only a few yards away. Up close, it was easy to see the horrible damage the *Sea Princess* had inflicted. Huge holes had been ripped through the decks, barrels were smashed and broken, and the mainmast lay in two pieces, the sail blackened and burning. Scattered here and there among the debris were what appeared to be small piles of rags. Catherine realized they were fallen men. Her throat tightened.

A horde of angry and dirty men stood at the railing as they tossed large iron hooks at the *Sea Princess*.

"They're boarding us!" Smythe yelled.

Derrick barked orders and soon the crew was at the ready, loaded pistols in hand. There was a horrible yell and a loud thud as the two ships finally came alongside, and then the pirates swarmed the deck.

Catherine's heart was beating so hard she could barely think. But a low moan from Lucas focused her. She had work to do. She opened his shirt and winced at the sight of the gash that had opened across his chest. Without thought, she pulled his shirt free, ripped it into long strips, and began to bind the wounds.

The smoke thickened and Catherine coughed in the billowing white clouds, her eyes stinging. She glanced up to see that one of the sails had caught on fire. Flames licked at the blackened edges, pieces of rigging dropping in red-hot pieces to the deck.

One short length of rope, burning on both ends,

dropped on top of Lucas. The boy cried out and Catherine grabbed the rope in the center where no fire crackled. She tossed it aside as the flames licked at her fingers. "We must get below deck!" she gasped.

Lucas moaned. "I—I can't move. Please . . . go without me."

"No." Catherine grabbed him under his arms and began to pull. Though he was only thirteen, he was heavy and it took all of her strength to drag him through the narrow opening between the barrels.

All around them men fought. With pistols, swords, and knives. The crew of the *Sea Princess* battled their enemy with a fury that had no equal.

"Ah, there ye be!" came a low, gravelly voice just a few feet behind Catherine. "I win the prize."

She whirled around and there, a sword in one hand, a smoking pistol in the other, was a pirate. He was taller than she was, with a wild black beard and narrow, black eyes. His shirt was torn and dirty, his pants stiff with grime. Catherine could smell him even over the horrible odor caused by the burnt tar and acrid smoke.

Catherine found Derrick's pistol and pulled it free. She leveled it at the pirate. Her heart pounded in her ears, but she managed to speak without quavering. "Don't come any closer."

A slow, sneering smile touched the pirate's hard face. "Ye wouldn't use that. Not a dab of a gal like ye."

"Try me," Catherine said steadily. She pointed the gun at the man's chest.

The pirate held up a warning hand, an ingratiating smile on his greasy face. "There now, there's no need to—" He lunged for her, his hand closing over the gun.

There was a sharp retort and the pirate suddenly arched forward, his eyes widening. He was so close that Catherine could smell his foul breath, feel his dirty hand over hers.

Then the pirate's eyes dropped closed and he fell into a lifeless heap. For a stunned minute, she looked down at him. Then she scrambled away, and hunched to the deck. Tremors shook her and she wrapped her arms about her knees, holding tightly, praying that this moment would soon be over. Something made her look up. Derrick stood at the edge of the foredeck, a smoking blunderbuss in his hands.

"Miss . . . Markham?" Lucas asked weakly.

Catherine tore her gaze from Derrick. She would not let him down. The battle was not yet won and there were things she could do to help. "Don't speak. You've lost a lot of blood."

"I . . . can you . . . I'm so . . . thirsty." He ran his tongue over his dry lips.

"I'll get you some water very soon." He looked so young, so fragile. A slow anger seeped through her at the monsters who would try to harm such an innocent boy.

All around her the battle raged, though it was clear that the crew of the *Sea Princess* had the advantage. From what Catherine could see, only three of them had been injured in the cannon fire, while many of the pirates had been wounded or killed.

The crew soon had the pirates on the run. They had managed to cut the lines from the grappling hooks and the two ships were now drifting apart. Seeing this, some of the pirates turned and ran, jumping the increasing distance to make it back to their ship. Some even tumbled into the rough sea, willing to swim in the violent ocean rather than stay aboard the *Sea Princess*.

Catherine gave a sigh of relief when Smythe appeared. She wasn't sure if it was the tossing of the ship or the sight of all the blood on Lucas's shirt that was making her queasy.

The first mate regarded the now unconscious boy. "How's the lad?"

"Not well. He's lost a lot of blood. I tried to stop it, but—"

Smythe uttered an oath under his breath and frowned. "Where is the physic when you need him?" He stood and looked around. "Ah, there he is, tending Marley."

"Is he injured?"

"Just a shot to the leg. He'll be up and about in no time. Lucas here is the worst of the lot. Masters! Bransom!

Come and take Lucas down to the galley so that Little can tend him."

"Little?"

"Aye, miss. Cook is also our physician."

Catherine stilled the uneasy beating of her heart. She hauled herself to her feet despite the pain in her ankle. "Bring Lucas to the captain's cabin. There's more room there."

Smythe shook his head. "I don't think we could—"

"Do as she says," came a deep voice. Derrick stood behind Smythe, his shirt black from soot, a cut on one cheek. He seemed to have escaped injury and Catherine became aware of a flood of relief.

Derrick looked down at the fallen pirate, then at Lucas. Finally, he cast a grim eye toward Catherine. "I thought I told you to stay hidden."

"I did," Catherine said. "He found us."

"I saw the man, Cap'n," Smythe said. "He was peering behind all the barrels and the like. He must have seen Miss Markham on deck before ye hid her."

Derrick didn't look convinced, but he said nothing more. Catherine felt the sting behind her eyes. The fight was over and her nerves were strung so tightly that she feared she'd burst into tears.

She blinked rapidly and tried to focus on the bustle about her. The ship looked far different from two days ago. Before, she'd felt a certain sense of satisfaction every time she saw the neatly scrubbed deck. Everything was always as it should be—every rope in its place, every barrel tightly lashed, every sail set just so, the wood so clean it shined. In the place of the order was chaos. The deck was covered with splintered wood, burned pieces of canvas, and traces of blood.

She would have thought the ship would have been hung with silence, the men quiet after such a horrid event. Instead, they hummed with talk, the thrill of the battle still strong, though one or two men glanced at Lucas, their bravado faltering at the sight of the blood that soaked the boy.

Catherine cleared her throat. "Did we . . . did we lose many men?"

Something dark passed before Derrick's gaze. "No, though three are grievously injured."

"And the pirates?"

"At least a dozen. One or two may still be alive."

Two men came to take Lucas below deck, stirring the boy to consciousness. He moaned as the men lifted him from the deck. Derrick stopped them and placed his hand over Lucas's, oblivious to the blood. "Get well."

Lucas managed a faint smile and then the men took him below.

A sudden surge of pity welled in Catherine's heart as she watched Derrick—he felt responsible for all of them, every person on the ship. He turned toward her, his gaze haunted. "Go below and see if you can help him. Lucas is . . . he's important."

She placed her hand on Derrick's cheek and forced her quivering lips to smile. "I'll do what I can for him. You do what you can for the rest of the crew."

He placed his hand over hers and nodded. "I will. Thank you, Catherine."

She stood there, her hand warm beneath his, her heart aching at the horror of the last hour. She wanted to lean forward, to throw herself in Derrick's arms, to give way to the tears that burned in her eyes. But she didn't. And she refused to appear weak in front of Derrick. Especially not after he'd kissed her.

He probably didn't even remember doing it . . . but Catherine remembered.

She nodded. "I'll go and see if I can assist with Lucas." Without another word, she turned and left, gritting her teeth against the pain of her sprained ankle as she picked her way down the ladder.

CHAPTER EIGHT

Lucas was quickly installed in Derrick's spacious cabin. Catherine hurried to spread a clean blanket on the bed even as she wondered at the events of the last hour. It seemed unreal and she felt numb, almost removed from the task she faced.

As soon as the men placed Lucas on the bunk, Little arrived. He was covered with grime and soot. Catherine frowned at the sight of the blood that soaked the front of his shirt.

"'Tisn't mine," he said cheerily, bending over the bed to examine Lucas. "I've been working on the other men."

"How many were injured?"

"A number of gunshot wounds, knife slashes, and the like. The worst is Poole, the bos'n's mate. He took a large wooden splinter to his leg."

And only that morning Poole had been showing Catherine around the ship. Her stomach clenched at the thought.

Smythe tsked. "Will he lose his leg, do ye think?"

"Lud, no, though 'tis likely he'll not get full use of it back." Little stripped the blood-soaked bindings from

126

Lucas's narrow chest to reveal a long gash.

Smythe peered over his shoulder. "Is it bad?"

"Reckon I'll need to wrap it." Little picked up the dirty strips of linen he'd just dropped on the floor. "This'll do. I'll just dab on some liniment and—"

"Oh, no, you don't," Catherine said, plucking the dirty linen from his hand. "This is filthy. You can't use it to wrap his wounds."

"Why not? 'Tis his, after all." The cook looked down at his own shirt, which was none too clean either. "I ain't going to use me own clothin', if that's what yer thinkin'. I've only this shirt and one other and I'm not about to—"

"Smythe, please run to my room and fetch the petticoat you procured for me in Boston."

The first mate appeared befuddled. "Yer petticoat? Miss Markham, I can't be touching your private linens."

"Fetch it," she replied in a firmer tone. "Lucas needs it."

Smythe turned a bright pink but off he went. A moment later he returned holding a white linen and lace petticoat at arm's length.

"Thank you," Catherine said, her arms and legs feeling leaden, as if she were moving through water. She took the petticoat and forced her stiff fingers to tear it into shreds.

"He will die if that wound gets infected," explained Catherine at the disbelieving look Smythe gave her. "It is important to keep him as clean as possible."

"Nonsense," Little huffed. "A little dirt never hurt no one."

Catherine ignored him. She crossed impatiently to the small table beside Derrick's bunk and poured some water from the pitcher into the washbasin.

Little scratched his nose. "What's that fer?"

"To wash his wounds." Catherine knelt by the bed, the two men automatically giving her room. She dipped one of the scraps of petticoat into the water, then carefully bathed the wound. "It's not as bad as I feared," she remarked on seeing the shallow but long cut that criss-crossed his narrow chest.

"'Tis bad enough." Smythe grunted, shaking his head. "Infection could set in, it could. I seen a man once't with no more cuts than this who swelled up like a pig and—"

"Smythe," Catherine said hastily, noting how Lucas's lashes trembled. So far, the boy had bravely held back his cries of pain. "Lucas does not need to hear about your friend's unfortunate circumstances. I daresay no one cleaned your friend's wounds, which we are going to do right now."

"Clean them?" Little said with a disgusted snort. "I haven't time. I jus' slather them with liniment and wrap them up tight."

"Hmph," Catherine said. No wonder people thought it was dangerous to live at sea. "What we need is whiskey."

Symthe's eyes brightened. "I can find some o' that!" He went straight to Derrick's desk, opened the second drawer down and brought out an amber bottle. He handed it to Catherine.

Little glanced uneasily at the door. "Ye shouldn't be getting' into Cap'n's whiskey, Smythe."

"Nonsense!" The first mate rubbed his hands together, his eyes gleaming. "'Tis medicinal. In fact, I was jus' thinkin' that I could use a leetle wet one, meself." He reached for the bottle, but Catherine kept it out of his reach.

"It's not for drinking. It's for cleansing."

His face fell, but after a heavy sigh and a longing glance at the bottle, he nodded.

She leaned over the injured cabin boy. "Lucas," she said softly.

His eyes fluttered open. "Miss Markham." Husky with pain, his voice threaded out in a whisper. "I don't want to die."

"You won't," she said with far more certainty than she felt. "I'm going to pour some whiskey over your wounds. It will hurt, but it will keep you from getting an infection."

The boy's pale gray gaze went from her to the bottle, then back. He gulped a breath, then nodded manfully. "Very well, miss. Do as ye must."

Little snorted derisively. "This is too much fer me. I'm the one as has experience."

"Hush, Little," Smythe replied. "Let Miss Markham

tend to Lucas. She knows what she's doing."

Catherine could only hope that was true. Truthfully, most of what she knew she'd learned from helping Haskins, the head groom at High Hill, in the barn with the animals. She closed her eyes and said a quick prayer, then tilted the bottle over the boy's chest. The second the liquid hit the bloody skin, Lucas arched in pain, his entire body rigid, his face twisted. He gasped, then went limp, his face pale, a damp line appearing on his forehead and upper lip.

"That should do it," Catherine said with surprising firmness. Her voice might not have trembled, but her hands did. She clasped them in her lap for a moment before ripping the petticoat into even more strips.

Between them, she and Little managed to wrap Lucas's wounds. Every move they made caused the boy excruciating pain, but they kept it up. As soon as they finished, Lucas gave a sigh of relief, offering Catherine a tremulous smile that warmed her through and through.

The door to the cabin opened and Derrick strode in. Catherine was immediately aware that the cabin seemed smaller, dwarfed by Derrick's broad shoulders.

He came directly to the bunk, his dark eyes flickering over Lucas's pale face. "How is he?"

Little said grumpily, "If he dies, I will be first to tell ye it wasn't my fault."

Smythe snorted. "And if he lives, ye'll be the first to

take the credit. Admit it. Miss Markham did a fine job bandaging up the lad."

"I ain't saying she did a bad job of it. But it will take more than a bandage to get him up on his feet. A little of me special tonic and ye'll never know he was injured."

Lucas's mouth thinned to a straight line. "I'd rather die than drink that foul concoction."

"So ye say," the cook said, pulling a small vial from his pocket. "Ye'll drink it or I'll force it down yer paltry throat, see if I don't."

The cabin boy gripped the thin blanket and held it before him like a shield, seeming to gather strength by the moment. "It'll take more than one of ye, fer I'll not open me lips for that sickening concoction!"

Catherine caught Derrick's gaze. He offered her a grin and said in a low voice, "Little's tonics are legendary among the men."

"What's in them?"

"From what I've heard, dirty dishwater and mud, though I wouldn't be surprised to discover there's some vinegar in there, too."

She glanced at the muddy-looking tonic and shuddered. "Ugh."

"That's putting it mildly. Lucas is right; I'd rather die than have to drink it."

Smythe leaned over to whisper. "I think Little makes it

taste foul on purpose, to force everyone to climb out of the sickbed all the quicker."

"It works," Derrick said.

"I heard that," the cook said, sending a dour glance at the first mate. "And it ain't true. 'Tis a secret tonic o' me granny's. And it will heal all manner of ills, which ye would know if ye'd but give it a try."

"I already gave it a try," Smythe said hotly. "Last year when I had a touch o' the ague." He placed a hand on his round paunch. "As sick as I was, I'd have rather been starved an' beaten than drink that poison again."

"Ye were happy enough to take it when I brung it to ye," Little said sourly.

"That was afore I tasted it." Smythe looked at Lucas with real pity in his eyes. "Mayhap ye don't need Little's tonic now that Miss Markham has bandaged ye up proper."

Lucas nodded weakly. "Aye, that's right. I don't need no more tendin' now that Miss Markham has seen to me."

Little went red in the face. "Well! That's gratitude fer ye!" He grabbed the vial and stuffed it into his pocket, then marched to the door. "I'll just go on back to the galley. That is, I will if ye think I'm fit to make yer rations!"

"Oh ye're fit fer that," Smythe said. "Just not fer doctorin'."

The cook harrumphed and stomped out, slamming the door behind him.

Derrick cocked a brow at his first mate. "We'll be eating pig's swill for a week at least."

"Oh, he'll calm down afore then," Smythe said with a grin. "Just to make sure of it, I'll challenge him to a game of cards and let him win. That always puts him in a better mood."

"See that you take care of it before dinner."

"Aye, Cap'n. How are things on deck?"

"There weren't as many repairs as I expected, though some of our sails are done for."

"I'll set the crew to mending 'em right away."

Catherine pulled the blanket more snugly about Lucas's thin shoulders. The boy smiled a bit woozily and closed his eyes. "Perhaps we should leave Lucas alone so he can sleep," she said to the men.

"The poor tyke," Smythe said in a loud whisper. He opened the door, then paused. His face reddened somewhat as he said, "Miss Markham, Lucas owes his life to ye. I'm . . . I'm glad ye're here."

Catherine managed a smile, though she knew her cheeks were as pink as his. "Thank you, Mr. Smythe. I'm glad I'm here, too."

He ducked a quick nod her way and then left.

Now that they were alone, Catherine found that she couldn't meet Derrick's gaze. Thoughts of the brief kiss he'd given her on the deck flooded through her. Had it really happened? Had she really felt his lips on hers? She

swallowed nervously and busied herself by picking up the
dirty rags that lay on the floor and putting them beside the
door. Lucas's even breathing told her that he was sleeping.

"I have to agree with Smythe," Derrick finally said, his
voice low. "You were very brave today."

"I didn't do anything as brave as the others."

"I don't know about that." Derrick came to stand
beside the bunk. He looked down at the thin boy, a crease
between his brows. "Smythe is right about one thing; if
you hadn't been there to see to Lucas—"

"Someone else would have. Derrick, those men put
their lives at risk. I could do no less."

A faint smile touched his mouth, but it didn't quite
reach his eyes. "There are times when you sound far too
much like your brother."

"Royce . . ." Catherine almost smiled at the thought of
her brother's outrage if he'd heard such a comment, but
somehow the smile wouldn't come. It stuck solidly in her
chest, pressing against her heart, keeping her from breathing.

Where was Royce now, she wondered. Alone? Afraid?
Did he believe they were not sending the money to secure
his freedom?

Derrick's warm hand closed over Catherine's. "We'll
find him, Catherine. I promise."

"How do you know? How do you know he isn't . . ."
Dead. But somehow, the word wouldn't come out. Her
entire body was suddenly overcome with exhaustion and

she pressed a shaking hand to her forehead.

Derrick gazed at Catherine's bent head, and the tightness that had knotted itself between his shoulders since the beginning of the battle suddenly released. He knew the pain of losing a loved one and he would be damned if he would allow Catherine to suffer. "Catherine, you have to trust me. I know all about men like this. I know about selfishness and greed." He placed a finger beneath her chin and lifted her face. Stark sadness darkened her gaze. "Whoever has captured Royce will keep him alive for no other reason than the fact that you are on your way with the gold."

Tears filled her green eyes. "I hope you are right," she whispered.

He smiled, sliding his hand over her cheek. Her hair was tangled about her face and a black smudge ran across one cheek. Her eyes were haunted, her face pale beneath the dirt. Never had she seemed more beautiful or more out of his reach. She was Catherine Markham, of the finest family he knew, while he . . . he was nobody. A fool who had made more mistakes in his short life than most men twice his age.

If Catherine knew the truth about him, knew what he'd done in his past, she'd back away from him, horror in her eyes. Just as his own mother had done when she'd faced the truth.

He closed his eyes against the pain of that memory.

She'd later come to understand, and had even forgiven him—yet he'd never forgotten her expression.

But, he told himself almost fiercely, Catherine didn't know his past. By some miracle, no one had told her why Derrick St. John was a black mark on the face of his family's honor. Why no one but Royce trusted him to serve as ship's captain. For the moment, she only knew him as her brother's friend. And for now, that was enough.

The realization freed him and something happened. He hadn't meant to touch her, to reach for her. But he did. One moment, he was standing looking down at her, marveling at her strength, relieved that she didn't know his past. And the next minute he was holding her against him.

She melted against him, her face buried against his shirt. Tremors shook her and he tightened his hold. "Catherine," he murmured into her hair. "Everything is fine."

"I—I can't seem to stop shaking," she said, her voice muffled against him.

"I know. It's common after a battle." He rubbed her back gently, savoring the feel of her in his arms. "Just relax. It has been a difficult week for all of us, but especially you."

Derrick remained where he was, holding her tight, letting her draw strength from him. She fit him perfectly, her chin just beneath his jaw. Derrick remembered their kiss earlier, just before the battle raged. He wanted to protect her, to save her.

From the bed, Lucas stirred, mumbling a little in his sleep. Catherine gave a little sigh and then stepped out of Derrick's embrace. "Thank you. I'm fine now."

"I'll have Little bring you something hot to drink. It will calm your nerves."

She cleared her throat. "I—I didn't mean to throw myself in your arms. It won't happen again."

Derrick rubbed a weary hand over his face. The events of the last few days weighed heavily on him. Catherine was but a dream . . . a far-fetched, romantic dream. Derrick sighed. "I need to return to deck. Catherine, I . . . Call if you need help with Lucas."

"Of course." She turned away to tuck the blanket in more securely about Lucas. Where her long hair was pulled to one side, the delicate nape of her neck was exposed.

Derrick didn't trust himself to stay a moment longer. He turned and left, striding quickly out to deck.

CHAPTER NINE

An hour later, Derrick glanced up at the sky. Their luck had held, and the storm hadn't unleashed itself on them. Not yet anyway. The sky was looking worse, though, inky black with an odd light.

"Let's take her closer to shore, Smythe," Derrick said as the first mate climbed the ladder to the foredeck.

"Aye, Cap'n," the first mate answered immediately, issuing orders in a brisk tone.

Derrick looked up at the tall masts and thanked the stars the rain had held off. It would have complicated matters to no end. Two of the mainsails had been lowered. One was blown to smithereens—it would have to be replaced. The other merely had some large rips in it where cannon shot had passed through, which could be patched. The sound of hammering and the creak of the riggings as they were being repaired filled the air. The men bustled about, calling to one another, their voices lighthearted. Word had apparently already spread that Lucas would be well.

"Cap'n?"

Derrick turned to find Smythe beside him. "Aye?"

"Marcus said there's two prisoners who're able to talk. Do ye wish to speak to them afore we lock them below deck?"

"Of course." Derrick followed the first mate to where two men sat tied back to back. They were ragged and thin, obviously underfed and overworked. One of them, the bolder of the two, had an evil-looking scar that ran the length of his face, splitting one eyebrow and ending in a wicked patch of puckered skin on his cheek.

Derrick met the man's gaze squarely. "Who are you?"

Neither prisoner said a word. Derrick gave an impatient curse. "You'll answer me or take a walk into the sea."

The smaller of the two men shifted uneasily, glancing at the ocean where it roiled like a live snake. After a moment, he returned his gaze to Derrick. "There's nothin' to tell."

"Indeed?" Derrick looked down at them, sorting through his own thoughts. "Do you know who I am?"

The larger man grinned widely. "Derrick St. John, son of a coward and a traitor." He spat, the glob of spittle landing between Derrick's boots.

It took every ounce of strength Derrick possessed not to lash out. As it was, only two things held him—the fact that the men were tied and the knowledge that a reaction—any reaction, would brand the comment as truth. "You blasted fool," Derrick managed to say after a moment. "I wouldn't sully the deck of my ship with your blood."

The thinner man swallowed so noisily it sounded like a gulp. "Ye . . . ye fought a good battle."

"The *Sea Princess* has been in several sea battles." He crossed his arms and rocked back on his heels, letting the roll of the ship slide through him. "But in all the sea battles I've been in, I've never seen a pirate ship waste time on an apparently empty vessel. Why did you attack?"

The bigger man's mouth clamped into a straight line and he stared straight ahead, but the other prisoner appeared uneasy. Derrick focused his efforts on him. "Just what did you hope to gain?"

For a moment, it appeared as though he would get no answers; both men appeared as sullen as clams. But a sound came up the gangway and Little arrived, carrying two plates of steaming stew, the tempting scent wafting with him. Both men's eyes lit up, and the smaller one even groaned a little.

Smythe leaned forward and took an appreciative whiff. "Aye, and it tastes as good as it smells. There's no ship in the whole ocean with a cook like ours. 'Tis almost a sin to eat, it tastes so good."

The cook seated himself on a barrel, the wooden trencher held just at nose level with the prisoners. "I've a whole pot o' this and more," he announced cheerfully. "Those as comes aboard the *Sea Princess* eats like kings, they do. Even prisoners."

Smythe eyed the trencher with avid interest, unconsciously rubbing his stomach. He leaned toward Derrick. "Cap'n, if the prisoners wish to walk the plank instead of eatin', can I have their servings?"

"Walk the plank or eat?" the larger prisoner said, his frown making the scar appear more menacing. "What kind of choice is that?"

"An easy one," Derrick replied. "Answer a few questions and have your supper. Or die. The decision is yours."

The thinner man opened his mouth eagerly, but his stern-faced companion interrupted. "We'll not say a word! Not one single word!"

"There ye have it, Cap'n." Smythe gave a satisfied sigh and reached for a plate. "No sense in wastin' good food."

Little held the trencher out of reach. "Oh no ye don't! Ye'll get yers when the time comes. This is for the prisoners."

"But they're goin' to walk the plank," Smythe said in a reasonable tone. "They won't need their supper."

"Oh," Little said, appearing struck by such logic. "Well. If ye think they won't be eatin' it, I suppose ye can—"

"I'm not goin' to walk no plank," piped up the thinner prisoner. He tried to twist in his bonds to glare at his companion. "Don't ye say another word fer me, Rogers. We was caught fair and square, and 'tis lucky we are not swimming the deep right now."

"Blast ye, Carpenter, ye traitor."

"I'm no more a traitor than ye. But I've no loyalties to the cap'n, and besides, I'm starvin'." He faced Derrick. "What do ye want to know?"

Derrick fixed a hard stare on the man. "You knew the *Sea Princess* was empty."

"Aye, but the cap'n didn't care. Right afore we sailed, he got a missive. I heard him arguing with the first mate about it."

Derrick stilled. Someone had notified the pirate ship that they were coming? "You were ordered to attack us?"

"Aye, Cap'n. We even let two prime frigates pass us by until we seen ye comin'. I heard Cap'n ask specifically if the coxswain could make out yer figurehead just to make certain 'twas ye and none other."

Good God, why would anyone be searching for the *Sea Princess* if not to steal her cargo? Derrick looked at his captives. "Who was your captain?"

The prisoner wasn't paying Derrick any more heed, his entire attention fixed on the stew plate.

Derrick leaned forward until he was in the line of sight between the stew and the prisoner. "The name of your captain, sailor."

The other prisoner twisted in his ropes. "Don't tell them a thing, Carpenter!"

But Carpenter was already lost in the spicy scent of the mutton stew. "Marler was our captain. Roger Marler. May I eat now?"

Derrick stiffened. Marler was a known pirate, riding the waves from the farthermost tip of America and back, preying on whatever ships he found and pillaging and murdering any who defied him.

But Marler did not work alone. He was one of many who answered to a man by the name of DeGardineau. And it was DeGardineau that Derrick had sworn to track down.

DeGardineau had once sailed the seas as first mate beneath Derrick's father. And it had been his testimony that had labeled Derrick's father a British sympathizer and a traitor.

"Cap'n?"

Smythe stood at Derrick's elbow, a concerned look on his face. "Perhaps we should see what else they know."

"They won't know anything else. Marler keeps all of his men in the dark. That way they can never double-cross him." Derrick nodded to the men holding the prisoners. "Let them eat. When they finish, lock them in the hold. We'll turn them over to the authorities once we reach land."

"Aye, Cap'n!" the men answered.

Derrick returned to the foredeck, Smythe close behind him.

"Do ye think DeGardineau sent the missive to Marler?"

"Who else?"

"Don't ye worry, Cap'n. We'll find the man who sullied yer father's name. See if we don't."

Derrick nodded grimly. Thunder rumbled overhead and Derrick glanced up. "It's going to rain soon. We're close enough to the coast now to miss the worst of it, but it will be a rough crossing."

"Aye, Cap'n." Smythe shook his head. "Ye don't need trouble like DeGardineau, not when ye're off to Savannah to rescue the lassie's brother."

Derrick lifted his face to the wind. It lifted in a cold rush, sending a heavy wave against the starboard side. The deck lifted and then dropped down. "Lower the sails. We'll ride her out right where we are."

Smythe began to turn toward the railing, halting halfway. A frown marred his broad face. "Cap'n, how could DeGardineau know we were on our way to Savannah? Ye didn't tell the crew 'til we were under way."

"I don't know, Smythe. That is what bothers me."

A cry went up from some of the men who were struggling to get a torn sail untangled from rigging that had suffered from the worst of the cannon fire. "Lord love them, but I'd best go and see if I can straighten out that mess," Smythe said, sighing. He waddled toward the ladder.

"Don't say a word of your thoughts to the men. If someone sent that ship after us, they might try again before we reach Savannah."

"Aye, Cap'n." Smythe left the foredeck, calling orders as he went.

Derrick watched the men working to clear the deck before the storm struck. Smythe was right—no one knew the *Sea Princess* was traveling to Savannah. But one person did know that Savannah was Catherine's destination. Namely, her uncle.

Could he have been behind the attack? If so, then Elliot Markham was indeed a man to be reckoned with, for he obviously held Catherine's safety in little regard. The thought disturbed Derrick. To still his mind, he restlessly left the foredeck and then climbed down to help the men with the torn sail.

The wind yanked on the ragged canvas and further tangled the broken lines. Derrick didn't say a word to them, but hauled himself up the rigging and began to climb to where the sail was caught. The wind rocked the ship fiercely, but he held tight and looped an arm about the mast. Derrick pulled his knife free from his belt and cut the tangled lines. The sail dropped and the men below gave a cry of triumph as they hurried to get the sail below deck for repair.

Derrick replaced his knife and swung himself down the rigging to the deck. His boots had just touched the planks when a movement flittered along the edge of his gaze. He turned his head in time to see Catherine coming toward him.

He looked at her, then looked again. The minx was

wearing one of his best shirts over a pair of breeches. She'd had to roll up the sleeves and it trailed down her to mid-thigh, blessedly covering most of her in the process. Derrick didn't think he'd ever seen his shirt worn to such advantage.

She paused by one of the men who was standing against the bulkhead, his leg bandaged at the knee. Catherine asked him a question and the man grinned from ear to ear. Derrick could just make out the man's words as he quipped about being too thick-skinned to let a little thing like a lead ball put him to shame. Catherine laughed.

The sound danced across the deck and the men slowed in their jobs to nod her way. His men looked at her differently now. She was no longer regarded with suspicion; she'd proved her worth and was another member of the crew.

She bade farewell to the man and continued on her way toward Derrick. He glanced around and found a bucket filled with nails and a hammer. He grabbed it up and took it across the deck to where some broken railing hung loose. He'd not worship at Catherine's feet the way his crew had decided to do. She'd have enough masculine admiration once they freed Royce and returned to Boston. The thought did not make Derrick any happier, and he hit the nails with far more force than necessary.

Worse, though he should have been focusing on his efforts to repair the railing, he couldn't help but steal glances as her as she approached. She'd washed and tied back her hair, though the wind had loosened some of the strands. She was a woman grown, every inch of her.

Derrick frowned to himself. She would be shocked if she knew his thoughts, for she saw him as nothing more than a friend of her brother's. He grit his teeth and yanked loose a broken piece of railing, then stripped the bent nails from it and tossed them into a waiting bucket.

"Derrick?"

He couldn't look at her—not now. What had brought her to his side, anyway? She had to know the effect she had on him. Or perhaps . . . perhaps she didn't. Catherine was a strange mixture of innocence and determination, a combination that was very difficult to resist.

"Derrick?" she asked again, a touch of impatience in her voice.

"What?" He swung the hammer even harder, slamming a nail into the wood with one short blow.

"Lucas is awake. He has a slight fever, but he seems to be on the mend." Catherine pushed a tendril of hair behind her ear and wondered at the strange look on Derrick's face.

He picked up a piece of broken railing and pushed it into place. "Good. You shouldn't be above deck until we've gotten some of this damage cleared away. You could get hurt."

Catherine clamped her teeth together. Was he so reluctant to be in her presence he would banish her belowdeck?

"I'll watch where I walk." She picked up a handful of nails. "May I help?" Without giving him time to answer, she picked up an extra hammer from the bucket and finished the line of nails Derrick had started. His silent regard lasted so long that she finally turned to look at him. "What's wrong?"

He looked away. "Nothing. Where's that mutt of yours?"

"George is sleeping on the foot of the bunk in my cabin. I don't think he even woke during the pirate battle."

Derrick's mouth curved into a ghost of a smile. "Lucky dog."

She pulled some nails out of the bucket and examined them to make sure they were straight. It was difficult not to stare at Derrick's brooding profile. He suddenly rocked back on his heels and met her gaze.

"Catherine, there is something you should know. I spoke with some of the prisoners. The pirate ship was waiting for us."

"They knew we were on our way to Savannah."

Derrick nodded. "Someone wanted to stop you from saving your brother."

"Who would do such a thing?"

"There's only one person who stands to gain anything if Royce *and* you do not return home. Your uncle."

Catherine put the hammer back in the bucket and turned to look at the cresting waves. What Derrick had just told her made her mind spin. "You think . . . you think

Uncle Elliot sent that ship out to capture us?"

"She wasn't trying to capture us; she was trying to sink us. I know it sounds crazy, but it's the only thing that makes sense. If neither of you return home . . ." Derrick shrugged. "He will have it all."

"I can't believe that! Uncle Elliot would never do such a thing."

"He is the only one with something to lose if you succeed."

Catherine pressed her fingers to her temples. "If it's true Uncle Elliot was behind the attack, then it's my fault that Lucas was injured."

Derrick frowned. "Catherine, you cannot take the wrongs of your uncle as your own."

She sighed and leaned against the repaired railing, letting the fresh wind blow across her face. Derrick had to be wrong about Uncle Elliot. She simply could not believe her own uncle would be so cruel. There was nothing to be done now except rescue Royce. The ship lifted on a wave and then dropped, and Catherine had to smile. After they rescued Royce, maybe she could convince him to take her sailing. "I love the ocean."

Derrick looked surprised at her changed spirits, but after a moment he said, "So do I. The St. Johns have always been adventurers. It's in our blood."

She glanced at him curiously. "What will you do when you marry?"

That appeared to dumbfound him, for he said in a strangled voice, "When I what?"

"When you marry. What will you do with your family? You cannot be gone for months on end and still have a family."

"I hadn't thought about it. I suppose that, after a while, I will hire captains to man my ships."

"How many ships will you have?"

His lips curved in a smile. "Dozens."

Catherine could not look away from his mouth. The very mouth that had kissed hers. The memory flooded her cheeks with heat. "I hope you succeed."

"So do I." Derrick sighed, rubbing his hand across his jaw. "If your uncle is trying to stop us from reaching Savannah, then we must have a care."

"How?"

He looked tired, she noticed for the first time, faint circles under his eyes. And no wonder—with the fight and then seeing to the repair of the ship, she doubted he'd even bothered to eat. "Have you had your supper?"

Derrick glanced at her, his brows lowered. "No. Not yet. Why?"

"Come on." She stood. "Little made some mutton stew and it is excellent."

"No. Catherine, we need to talk."

"We can talk in your cabin while you are eating. In fact, I think you should go right now and—"

"If your uncle sent the pirates, then he has decided that you are expendable. His next effort won't be so gentle."

She stood, mouth open, trying to absorb this information. Uncle Elliot may not have lifted a finger to help Royce, but to think of him actively seeking to murder someone . . . "I know it looks that way, but Uncle Elliot would never do such a thing."

"Perhaps, but perhaps not. Catherine, think about it. If we are killed on our way to Savannah, then Royce will die and your uncle will inherit by default. In a way, you've given him more of an opportunity to gain it all by running off to save Royce on your own."

"I'm not alone," she said, still struggling to believe that Uncle Elliot could be so uncaring. "I have you."

His expression froze and heat rushed to Catherine's cheeks. Oh dear, she hadn't meant to say that. She managed a strained smile. "And George will protect me."

Derrick's expression darkened, but before she could respond he turned away. Had it been anyone else, she would have thought her flippant words had wounded his feelings. But Derrick wasn't that kind—he was as brash as her brother and he couldn't care less what she believed or felt.

She crossed her arms and shivered in the wind. "What do we do now?"

"Race like hell for Savannah and hope your uncle has not sent other ships as well."

It was so risky. She suddenly realized that it was entirely possible that the pirate ship could return to finish what it had started. And if it didn't, whoever it was who wanted to keep them from reaching Savannah might send another ship after them. "Derrick?"

He glanced at her, his gaze dark. "Yes?"

"Thank you." It wasn't much, but it was all she had to give. He was risking so much—his ship, his life, the lives of his men. All for her brother.

His expression softened and he reached over and flicked a careless finger over her cheek. "You and Royce would do the same for me," he said in a quiet voice.

"Yes, we would." She found his gaze locked on her and she gave him a tremulous smile. "I would, anyway. I shouldn't speak for Royce."

"He'll be able to speak for himself soon enough." Derrick brushed a strand of her hair from her face and for an instant, his hand hovered over her cheek. Before she could help herself, she leaned against him. He cupped her cheek, his warm fingers on her bare skin.

Catherine closed her eyes, savoring the feeling, enjoying the sudden quiet that seemed to engulf them. The moment lengthened. Neither she nor Derrick moved. A faint tremor shivered through Catherine and she lifted her face toward his.

Derrick dropped his hand. "Catherine, no."

His voice was harsh. Her heart fell with the hurt of it. "I just wanted—"

"You don't know what you want." He picked up the bucket of nails. "I've work to do. If we are to reach Savannah at all, the ship must be repaired, which will take a few days as it is. Meanwhile, you keep an eye on Lucas."

She managed a nod. "Of course. I—I should check on him now." With a heart choked with tears, she turned on her heel and hurried away, almost running in her haste. But what she was running from, she carried with her, for her heart ached with each step.

CHAPTER TEN

Elliot Markham was furious. Everything had gotten dangerously out of control. It had all seemed so simple, at first. It had been so easy, so neat and clean. But then Catherine had ruined everything.

"This is all Catherine's fault," Elliot muttered.

Life had forced him to make some ugly decisions, but it would not be in vain. He was now in Savannah, ready to finish the unpleasantness. He made his way up the street to the rickety house he'd been directed to. Elliot wrinkled his nose as the faint odor of stale cooked cabbage reached him.

He hated this place—hated any place that was not High Hall. After today, he vowed that nothing would pry him from his new home.

Two days after he'd sent DeGardineau's men after the *Sea Princess*, Elliot had received a very tersely worded note instructing him to present himself here, at this disreputable tavern, in Savannah. His first impulse was to haughtily refuse to come. By God, he was a Markham, and the Markhams bowed to no one.

But further reflection made him pause. Perhaps DeGardineau had some important information to impart.

What if . . . Elliot frowned. What if DeGardineau's men had been unable to halt the *Sea Princess*? Derrick St. John had quite a reputation as a master sea captain. Could he have escaped?

No. That was unthinkable. DeGardineau was a noteworthy captain in his own right. Perhaps it was something else. Had they located Royce's kidnappers? Could that be the problem?

His heart full of dread, Elliot decided to answer the rather peremptory summons. He'd much rather have sent someone else, but he dared not let anyone know of his association with such disreputable men.

Anxious to put the issue behind him, he had traveled to Savannah with all possible speed, though a part of him had detested every second of the trip.

Elliot knocked on the door. After a long silence, someone shuffled up and swung it open. A short, fat man with beady eyes stared up at him. "Ye're late."

Elliot didn't dignify this with a reply. He stepped past the man and into the entryway. The old man closed the door, then jerked his head toward an open door to their right. "In there." He didn't wait for Elliot to answer, but limped on down the hallway and disappeared from sight.

Suppressing an aggravated sigh, Elliot peered into the room. It was so dark that he halted a moment to let his gaze adjust. The room came slowly into focus. Low and dark, the stained ceiling sagged piteously. An assortment of broken chairs surrounded a table to one side of the small, smoke-stained fireplace.

Two men occupied the room. One was a small, nervous man with a scarred face and long, greasy hair. He stood beside the fire, shifting uneasily from one foot to the other. His reddish hair seemed strangely bright in the dingy room. Elliot noted the ivory handles of pistols sticking out from the man's wide belt, and an assortment of knives tied here and there. The fool was obviously a common thug.

Elliot glanced at the other man, and his attention was caught. Though equally dirty, he possessed the remnants of a shabby elegance. He wore a torn, wine-colored coat that had seen better days, with only two brass buttons remaining. A dirty kerchief was knotted about his throat and his black boots were badly in need of polishing. A jaunty black hat perched on his head, above long black tresses that shone with grease.

Elliot nodded briefly. "DeGardineau."

The man grinned, his teeth startlingly white in his dark face. "I have been waiting." A faint French accent colored his words.

"I came as soon as I got your missive. We must speak."

"*Oui*, we must. It seems you forgot to mention a few things about this ship that carried your niece. You told us the name of the ship and where you thought it would be.

But you failed to mention her captain."

Though DeGardineau's smile never slipped, Elliot felt the menace in his tone. He stiffened. "I didn't think it was important who manned the ship. All you wanted to know was her route."

"And any pertinent information that would affect the outcome of your little plan. Didn't you wish us to sink the ship that held your niece?"

"Of course." Elliot managed to keep his expression bland, though his anger simmered. "I want this matter taken care of."

The Frenchman rubbed his chin. "You want to stop the chit before she reaches Savannah."

"*Before* she can deliver the gold."

DeGardineau reared back in his chair, lacing his fingers over his stomach. His gaze was darkly amused, as if he knew something Elliot did not. "I wonder who holds your nephew prisoner?"

Elliot sat in the chair across from the Frenchman. "Haven't you found out yet? You are to make certain he is dead. His kidnappers will do the job for us if we can keep Catherine away."

"Ah, that would be convenient, no? Your nephew dies and your conscience is clear." DeGardineau leaned forward on his arms, a faint smirk on his face. "Or is it? You are a liar, *Monsieur* Markham."

That a common thug would dare speak to him, Elliot

Markham, in such a way! Elliot stood so abruptly that his chair toppled over.

Click. A cocked pistol was shoved against his head. The redheaded man had moved so quickly that Elliot had not seen him.

"Easy, *mon ami*," DeGardineau said, pouring himself another drink. "Marcel does not have the sense of humor I do. He would prefer to shoot first and ask questions later."

Elliot's chest ached with the pressure of his heartbeat. He waited until DeGardineau nodded to his henchman before he took the chair he'd abandoned and sat once again, rubbing his damp hands on his breeches. "I am a busy man, DeGardineau. What do you want? I don't have time for these games." He couldn't believe he'd agreed to come to Savannah. If he knew anyone else who could do what he wanted to accomplish . . . But he didn't and his hands were tied. "I thought you said you would be able to stop my niece. Did you?"

DeGardineau's gaze narrowed. "You did not tell me the ship belonged to St. John."

"What difference would that have made? He is a nothing, a has-been pirate and no more."

"Had I known it was St. John, I would have gone myself," he said quietly. "He and I have a matter to settle. And there is only one way it will end."

That was interesting indeed. Elliot rapidly tried to remember the rumors he'd heard about St. John. Derrick had always been a wild one, running off when he was still a lad, then turning to piracy. He was more successful than any other pirate, but that was not what made his name. What made him memorable was that he never lost a battle. Or so the rumors had gone.

Elliot's lip curled. He didn't believe in rumors. Most of St. John's success must have come from his reputation and not skill. After his first few successes, the remaining ships refused even to fight him, tamely handing over their bounty in exchange for safe passage. Sorry excuses for seamen, the lot of them, Elliot thought with disdain.

DeGardineau leaned back in his chair, his dark gaze flickering over Elliot. "You do not understand, *mon ami*. Once a pirate, always a pirate. He knows our ways, does St. John. And he used them to defeat my best captain, Marler."

Elliot shrugged. "That is not my problem."

"Ah, but it is. St. John damaged Marler's ship badly. He believes we owe him for our stupidity."

"I owe him nothing," Elliot said with a faint sneer.

The man beside the fireplace stepped forward again, his hand gripping his pistol. Elliot's own gun rested in his front pocket, but he took little comfort in it—it would take a moment to reach it and in that moment, death could claim him.

DeGardineau held up a hand. "Let him be, Marcel. He is our guest. Besides, St. John or no, Marler was caught unawares. There is no excuse for stupidity."

After a tense moment, Marcel stepped back and DeGardineau smiled. "You must forgive him. He has no patience."

Elliot managed a brittle nod. The thought of dying here, on the dirty floor of a hovel, was too horrible to dwell on. This was not how he was supposed to die. No, his life was to be filled with wealth and ease, with opportunity and victory. Yet it seemed that something was always standing in his way, preventing him from succeeding the way he longed to.

Unless this scheme worked. Elliot managed a tight smile. "We are arguing over nothing."

DeGardineau smoothed the dark mustache that dripped over his upper lip. "Are we?" He picked up an empty cup and wiped it on his sleeve, then splashed some liquid from a bottle into it and placed it in front of Elliot. The scent of rum rose from the cup, strong and sweet.

Elliot ignored the drink. He leaned forward. "We still have to deal with my niece. I do not want her to reach Savannah."

DeGardineau took a drink from his own glass, his gaze absently resting on Elliot's glass for a moment. "It will cost you."

Elliot reached into his pocket. Marcel's gun immediately moved to point directly at him. Elliot looked at

DeGardineau and slowly pulled out a small bag and placed it on the table. "I assumed you would require part of the payment up front."

DeGardineau's smile broadened. "Marcel! Put down the gun. *Monsieur* Markham is making a payment. How much is it?"

"Ten gold pieces."

"I will need ten more."

It was robbery. Elliot had already paid that much. But what could he do? Elliot forced himself to relax. He didn't like the way DeGardineau was smiling, as if he were amused by Elliot and his offer.

DeGardineau pulled open the bag and picked up one coin. He bit the edge of it. "A fine coin."

"It's a payment," Elliot snapped. He leaned forward. "My niece, DeGardineau."

The pirate tossed the coin back into the bag. He picked it up and tossed it to Marcel, who secured it out of sight in his coat. "Your niece—you want her . . ." He lifted a finger and drew a line across his throat.

Elliot watched him with a sense of horror. Seeing the filthy pirate making such a graphic gesture brought a touch of reality to what was happening. It had been one thing to ask DeGardineau to see to it that Royce never returned home. After all, he hadn't *specifically* asked the man to kill anyone. Therefore, Elliot was blameless. The same could be said about sending one of DeGardineau's ships after the *Sea Princess*. It wasn't as if Elliot had held a trigger to anyone's head.

But seeing DeGardineau's dirty finger pass across his throat sent a sick shiver through Elliot. It was horrible, but what else could he do?

He closed his eyes and took a deep breath. If Catherine managed to save Royce, all was lost. Elliot heard himself say, "Do what you must." He opened his eyes and found DeGardineau regarding him with ill-concealed contempt.

"*Monsieur* Markham has no stomach for blood."

"I have the stomach," Elliot replied stiffly. "But I cannot be connected with . . . the incident."

"The incident, eh? That's one way to put it."

"If there was any other way—" Elliot clamped his mouth closed. He didn't have to justify himself to this cretin. He didn't have to justify himself to anyone. "You may have to take care of that St. John character, too. I doubt he will just take Catherine to Savannah and leave her. He may have been a pirate once, but he has been in my nephew's employment for a while now. He may feel the need to stay with Catherine. He may even help her."

DeGardineau frowned. "St. John has ties with the girl?"

Marcel burst into speech, but since it was French, Elliot did not understand any of it. DeGardineau listened for a moment, then scowled, cutting his henchman off with a sharp gesture. He met Elliot's gaze and managed a shrug. "Marcel dislikes the thought of killing St. John. He says the man has many friends."

"And I have many gold pieces." At least he would, once Royce and Catherine were gone.

DeGardineau chuckled. "So you do." He said something over his shoulder to Marcel, who answered with a long spate of French.

"The gold reconciles Marcel to St. John's fate."

"Excellent. Do whatever you will, DeGardineau, but no one, not even the girl, is to know I had anything to do with this."

"Of course not," DeGardineau said with a flinty smile. "It wouldn't benefit me in any way to reveal your secrets."

Elliot thought there was a threat in those words, but surely not. After all, he was Elliot Markham, soon to be the wealthiest man in Boston, and DeGardineau was nothing more than a common thief.

"We are done, then." Elliot stood. "I expect a full report once you've finished."

"Of course. I will send you a message as soon as it is done." DeGardineau smiled broadly.

Moments later, Elliot emerged from the wretched house and blinked against the strong sunlight. He felt dirty somehow, as if a thin layer of filth had adhered to his skin. He would find a quality inn and request a bath. And soon he would go home. Elliot pictured the beautiful house on the hill that was almost his and he smiled, pushing aside a faint twinge of guilt. He deserved such a home. High Hall was his. Or would be very, very soon.

CHAPTER ELEVEN

Derrick wearily stretched his arms over his head. They should be in Savannah now, but they'd been forced to stop in a secluded cove to make some of the more urgent repairs. Thank goodness everything had gone smoothly and they hadn't been delayed more than two days. The crew seemed to appreciate the time to recover almost as much as the *Sea Princess*.

They sailed as soon as they were able. Derrick tried to stop his mind from racing over and over the events of the last week. He worried that whoever had sent the ship to attack them might return to finish the job.

It was almost eight in the morning, and he'd watched the entire night slide by from the foredeck, only just now stumbling back to his cabin. There had been no more attacks, not even a ripple on the still horizon. But that hadn't made him feel any better.

Something was wrong. He could feel it in the stillness of the night, in the silent lap of the waves against the ship. Derrick rubbed his eyes wearily, wondering how his friend was faring. Despite his calming words to Catherine, he wondered if Royce would still be alive when they reached him. He had to be.

Derrick turned on his heel, suddenly impatient to be doing something despite his sleepless night. *Anything* other than standing still, waiting. If he was going to save his friend, he would have to outmaneuver his pursuers. He had already laid a new course. He looked down at the chart that lay on the table and traced the line he'd plotted. Within the hour, they would move from their current position to the new course.

It was a good plan, solid and cautious. Instead of sailing along the coast as they usually did, they were heading directly out to sea. Once they were out a goodly distance, they'd turn and make their way south once more. They would never be visible by land and while it might take them a day or so longer to reach Savannah, it would be worth it to keep Catherine safe. And that was Derrick's first priority. Royce would agree that Catherine's safety came first.

Derrick opened a porthole and let some of the salty morning air ease into the cabin. He'd always longed for a cabin with a porthole from the moment he'd first taken to the sea. As a cabin boy with a rowdy group of sailors, all of them larger and more hardened than he, he had gotten the smallest portions of food, the worst shifts, and the dampest location to string his hammock.

He leaned his shoulder to the wall and looked back at his cabin. That had all changed now. He was a captain.

And of something more than a pirate ship.

"A pirate," he whispered, pressing his cheek to the cool wood porthole frame. It made his heart ache to remember those years. He had stolen and raided, battled and destroyed, all in the name of greed. Everything a pirate did was motivated by gold coin and little else. He rubbed his eyes again, wishing he could forget those years of his life.

Derrick hadn't set out to sea to become anything other than a sailor. When he'd been younger, he'd begged to go to sea with his father, but Captain St. John had wanted better for his son and he'd refused. At the time, it had seemed as if his father thought Derrick wasn't good enough to be a sailor.

To prove him wrong, he'd run away from home and joined the crew of a likely ship.

Derrick did so well that he was eventually promoted, raised to rank of bos'n's mate by the time he was sixteen. But then the ship was overtaken by pirates just off the Carolinas, and Derrick, along with twenty-one other members of the crew had been given an ultimatum—join the pirate crew or jump ship.

Only one man had jumped—Derrick and the rest of the crew had signed their names in blood on the ship's manifest. At first, it hadn't seemed all that different from being on a frigate; sea life was hard no matter where you were. Furthermore, the captain of the pirate ship was more democratic than most, offering to give shares of the plunder to each member who stayed with the ship. The men, too, were freer than Derrick had ever experienced, and he soon found the home he'd been missing since he'd left Boston.

Derrick sighed heavily, thinking back to the pirate attack from the day before. The pirate he'd shot had yelled something right before he'd lunged at Catherine . . . what was it?

Derrick closed his eyes, remembering the moment clearly, hearing the horrible sound of gunfire, smelling the smoke once again. He could almost see Catherine's expression. Derrick had been standing only a few yards away, his own gun ready. But just as he started forward, a swell of smoke had obscured her from his view and he'd been afraid to fire, afraid he'd hit Catherine and not the pirate. His heartbeat had been louder than the thunder of the cannons.

It was then that the man had called out something. Derrick frowned, the words suddenly echoing in his mind. *There you are. I've won the prize.* Derrick raked a hand through his hair. Won the prize? Had Elliot Markham put a price on Catherine's head?

It was chilling to think how close Elliot had come to succeeding. The thought made his stomach tighten.

He looked at his neatly made bunk, his eyes heavy. Lucas had asked to be moved to his own bunk this afternoon, pleading that he was more comfortable with his mates than holed up in the captain's cabin. Derrick had reluctantly allowed the lad his way.

A bone-weary tiredness seeped through Derrick. Perhaps he should rest just for a little while before going on deck. Sometimes he had his best thoughts while lying down. He undid his shirt and threw it over the desk chair, then laid down. Thoughts milled through his head as he thought over first one scenario, then another. But one by one, his thoughts quieted. And soon, exhausted beyond belief, Derrick St. John, captain of the *Sea Princess*, was sound asleep.

The sea was calm. Deadly quiet, like a black blanket of ink stretched before the cold moon. A chill wind filled the sails of the pirate ship, but didn't raise so much as a whitecap on the smooth, glassy water. Derrick knew he should have been cold, for his breath formed in a white cloud, but he was warm through and through.

A burst of red fire came from the distance, and the Sea Princess *lurched as cannon shot rang out. At his side, Catherine gasped, then screamed. He felt rather than saw the pirate boarding the ship. Felt rather than saw the pirate aim a pistol toward Catherine. Derrick whirled to shout a warning, but the pistol was quicker. Fire flared from the muzzle and Catherine staggered back. Her blond hair whipped about her stunned, pale face and a blossom of red stained her white shirt.*

Her gaze locked with his as she crumpled to the ground, tears slipping down her cheeks. Derrick reached her and lifted her into his arms. He

*looked into her eyes and read confusion and sadness . . . and love. Love—
for him. The thought astounded him. How could Catherine, destined
to become the wife of a wealthy man, a prosperous man, love him?*

*He had to tell her. Tell her that he loved her, too. But as he opened
his mouth, she sighed, her lashes closing over her green eyes.*

*She was gone. Her life robbed by the loud choke of a gun. Derrick
held her lifeless body as fury, raw and bitter, filled his heart. Derrick
stumbled to his feet, yanking his pistols from his belt. He turned and ran
toward the leering pirate. But when he faced the evil man, it wasn't a
pirate at all, but his own father—a smoking pistol still in his hand.*

The pirate's leer was suddenly a sad smile. "I'm sorry, son."

*Derrick brought his pistol up and cocked the hammer. "So am I." He
squeezed the trigger and—*

"Cap'n?" Symthe's voice broke into Derrick's dream.
"Are ye awake? Ye were thrashin' like the devil was
a-chasin' ye."

Derrick blinked hazily in the blaze of light that per-
meated the room, the dream still painfully fresh in his
mind.

Smythe stood at the foot of the bunk, a worried
expression on his face, a tankard in one hand. "Little sent
me to bring you this. Said ye told him ye couldn't sleep.
Guess he heard ye wrong."

"No, I couldn't sleep at all last night, but today . . ."
Derrick pushed himself upright and swung his feet over
the side of the bunk. "What time is it?"

"Six in the evening."

"Evening?" Derrick stood. "The ship! I was going to—"

"Now, now! Don't get in a natter, Cap'n! I came by this morning to check on ye and I found the chart on yer desk."

Derrick rubbed a hand over his face. "I didn't hear you come in."

"O' course ye didn't! I was as quiet as a mouse, I was. I'd have awakened ye, but ye were sleepin' like a babe, and I thought 'twas a sin to disturb ye."

"Did you change our course?"

"Just as ye wished."

Derrick managed a grin. "Next time, feel free to awaken me."

"Ye needed yer rest, Cap'n. We're all tired from doin' double watch." Smythe tilted his head to one side. "But, from the looks o' ye, sleep isn't as restful as it used to be. Ye were thrashing about a good bit."

"I dreamed—" Derrick looked away from Smythe's bright gaze. "I don't know what I dreamed."

"Nonsense! Ye must remember something."

"Not a thing."

Smythe watched as Derrick stood and crossed to the map. Lord help the boy, but Smythe hated to see the captain in such low spirits. In the twenty-one years he'd known Derrick St. John, Smythe had come to appreciate the solid nature of the boy who was now a full-grown man, with a demeanor far older than his years. It was sad the way the weight of responsibility had changed the carefree lad into such a somber adult. Somber and unapproachable.

But most of that rested with the rumors about the lad's father. The possibility that the old captain had betrayed his ship.

Smythe pursed his lips. "Cap'n, I know I've tol' ye this afore, but it seems to me that ye needs to hear it again. I had the privilege of sailing with yer father fer almost thirty years afore I sailed with ye. He was a good cap'n. One o' the best."

"Yes, he was."

"He was also an honest man. I don't believe what they say about him and ye shouldn't either. He'd have died afore he turned coat and attacked a ship from the colonies. He hated the British. There's no way he would have agreed to join them. He'd never commit treason."

"There were witnesses, Smythe. DeGardineau was a member of his crew. At the inquest, he testified that Father—"

The first mate snorted. "There are also people who swear their shoes were stolen by pixies."

Derrick's frown softened. "Pixies, eh?"

"Little told me the other day that he thought his salt shaker was possessed because ever' time he set it down, it would up and move." Smythe shook his head. "It'll make ye wonder at the sanity of the world to hear all the tales people will believe."

Derrick was quiet a moment, picking up the map and carefully rolling it and then storing it in a hollow metal tube. Finally, he said, "I don't want to believe my father did such a thing."

"Ye've naught to fear—I'd swear on me life that yer father would die afore he'd betray anyone."

The captain was silent a moment, then looked up with a frown. "Where is Miss Markham?"

"On deck. Peters is with her."

The captain went to the basin by his bunk and poured a small amount of water into it, splashing his face. Then he pulled on his shirt, leaving it undone for the moment. "We have to watch out for Miss Markham. It's possible danger awaits her in Savannah."

"I'll watch her with me life," Smythe replied honestly, following the captain out of the cabin and into the hallway. "She's a fierce one, is Miss Markham. Reminds me of me own mother, a resourceful woman she was."

Derrick climbed the short set of steps to the deck and lifted his face to the sun. Overhead the sky was a soft blue, nary a cloud in sight, the sun setting on the horizon. "'Tis a fine wind."

Smythe grinned and nodded, then stopped, his smile fading, his gaze locked on a spot on the mast high above their heads. "I declare, but I don't think Miss Markham should be up that high."

Derrick followed the first mate's gaze. There, high above the deck, climbing slowly, ever so slowly, up the rigging was Catherine. Bloody hell! "She'll be killed." Derrick strode forward. "Who is responsible for this?" he shouted.

Peters stood at the bottom of the mast, beaming proudly. "There ye be, Cap'n! We're showin' Miss Markham how to climb the rigging."

"Aye," piped up Bransom. "She's a natural, she is. Took to it like a fish to water."

Derrick forgot that climbing the rigging was something his crew did each and every day they sailed. Even he was known to climb occasionally, just to get a good look at the horizon and to feel the breeze. All Derrick could think of was that one tiny slip could mean Catherine's death.

Anger warred with concern and he opened his mouth to yell, when Smythe leaned over and said, "I wouldn't distract her now, Cap'n."

Peters nodded. "Lud, no! She'd fall for sure then."

Derrick was assailed with the image of Catherine's lifeless body for the second time that day. "I can't let that happen," he muttered, feeling helpless. It was, he decided, a feeling he did not like at all.

* * *

From high above the deck, Catherine placed her foot on a section of line and gripped the narrow beam above her head. With a quick motion, she hoisted herself onto the beam and straddled it, glad Peters had explained the benefits of climbing barefooted. She could grip with her toes, if need be.

She held on to the beam and felt the sway of the ship below. Though she had been aware of the motion of the sea, it seemed more pronounced up here. The masts seemed to sway back and forth like upside-down pendulums, the movement making her stomach faintly nauseated. "Not now," she muttered to her uncooperative belly. "We've only a bit more to go."

So up she went, each step taking her farther and farther. But the higher she went, the more the mast seemed to sway and the farther away the deck looked.

She was only about halfway up when her stomach began to demand that she climb back down. But with the expectant gaze of the entire crew on her, Catherine couldn't very well just quit. So she kept climbing, telling herself that it would get easier.

"It's not that hard," she said bracingly. "Even Lucas goes this high." She reached for the line above her head, reluctantly leaving her relatively safe perch on the beam. "Perhaps I should have reminded them that I am still sore from the battle. Or that I twisted my ankle on the ladder only two days ago. Or just that I am terrified of falling. But no—" Her foot slipped off a line and for an instant Catherine was hanging suspended above the deck, holding on for dear life.

A shout came from below, and Catherine glanced over her shoulder—then wished she hadn't. The deck looked far, far away. Catherine could see people peering up at her, but her head was swirling so much she couldn't make out any faces. The sight sent her stomach plummeting, and a faint sweat broke out on her brow.

"I'm going to die," she muttered, her feet flailing wildly as she sought purchase on one of the lines. And all because she'd let enthusiasm overcome logic. Her left foot hit something, and she realized with relief that it was a taut line. She put her weight on it and then wrapped her arms about the mast and hung on, pressing her cheek against the smooth wood. For an instant, she wondered what they would say about her if she never came back down.

"I really don't care what they think. 'Tis better to be a live coward than a dead one." If she fell, she'd never survive. She'd be flattened on the deck like one of Little's pancakes.

But if she wanted to get down, she would have to release the mast. To Catherine's chagrin, she found that she couldn't. Her hands clenched tighter and she hugged the mast fiercely.

How long she was there, she didn't know. But after

many long, long moments, a quiet voice very close by said, "Catherine."

It was Derrick. Catherine opened one eye and carefully peered down.

"Don't look," he commanded, his voice closer now. "Just hold on. I'll be there in a minute."

"Hurry!" Her hands were getting numb where she was holding on to the mast so tightly. If she got out of here alive, she'd *never* climb another thing, not even a footstool. "Can't you climb faster?"

"I'm almost there," he said, his deep voice reassuringly close.

She managed to open both eyes. Derrick's face appeared, his mouth set in a grim smile. "You fool. What did you think you were doing?"

"Climbing. Or I was, but then . . ."

"I can't believe you let them talk you into this."

"They didn't talk me into anything. I was so hoping they'd—" The ship lifted on the crest of a wave and Catherine scrambled to get closer to the mast, which was impossible as she was already plastered to it. "Ack!"

"Just hold on. I'll get you."

She closed her eyes and pressed her cheek to the wood. "I can't move."

"You don't have to. Not yet, anyway." He was beside her now, moving so that his body was against her.

Catherine soaked in the feel of him, of his strong legs against hers, his arms about her as he grabbed the mast just above her head.

"Just take a few deep breaths and, whatever you do, don't look down."

"I'm already breathing as deeply as I can and there's no way I'm going to look anywhere."

Amusement deepened his voice. "I'm afraid you're going to have to open those pretty eyes of yours if you want to make it back to the deck."

Catherine looked at him. "Pretty? You . . . you think my eyes are pretty?"

A grin lifted one corner of his mouth. "Your eyes are very pretty." He brushed a strand of her hair from her face with a gentle gesture. "Are you ready?"

She took a shuddering breath. "I'm as ready as I'm going to be."

"Good. I'm going to climb down and you are going to follow every move I make."

"I'll fall."

"If you slip, I'll catch you."

"And if you don't?"

A light simmered in the blue depths of his gaze. "You won't fall alone."

Shaking from head to toe, Catherine nodded.

Derrick swung over and placed his hand on the other side of the mast. He was completely covering her now, his arms to either side of her, his feet resting on the line below hers. "I'm going down now. Do exactly as I do." He moved to the next lower rung. Catherine swallowed. She was so frightened. But somehow, knowing Derrick was just a step away settled her stomach and gave her strength.

"Are you coming?" he asked.

She clung to the mast and tentatively searched for the line with one foot.

"Lower," he said.

She tried to find the line with her foot, but couldn't. "Derrick, I can't—"

"*Lower*," he said again, his voice so commanding that it jarred Catherine.

They didn't call him "Cap'n" for the fun of it, she decided. "I'm trying to," she replied in a testy voice. But she complied, nonetheless, stretching her foot until her toes brushed the line below. Cautiously, she edged her weight down to the line, sliding her hands along the mast as she lowered herself.

"Don't hang on to the mast like that. You'll get a splinter."

He was right. She forced herself to move back into the lines and away from the solid safety of the mast. "If I fall, I'm going to blame you."

"If you make it to the deck, I'm going to box your ears for taking such foolish chances. Now come."

She followed him, foothold for foothold, inching their

way down. He stopped once in a while and made a comment or recalled some tidbit about Royce. She knew he was trying to calm her, and she did nothing to stop him. Catherine lowered her foot to the next line and put her weight on it. For a second, she was fine. But then, as she put her weight on it, her foot slipped off.

Derrick was there in a heartbeat. "Don't let go!"

The line cut into her fingers where she clung to it, her feet swinging free. The ship creaked and swayed and Catherine prayed she wouldn't die.

"Hang on tightly and swing your feet to the right. Easy now."

She did as she was told, her toes brushing something. She found the line and carefully eased her weight onto it, her knees trembling.

Derrick moved to stand with her, his arms to either side of her. "Are you all right?"

It was heavenly to hear the concern in Derrick's voice. He may have only seen her as the younger sister of his best friend, but he genuinely cared what happened to her. For the first time since Royce had set sail and never returned, Catherine didn't feel alone. She knew that whatever perils lay ahead, she would be the stronger for having Derrick by her side.

"We've only a little more to go," Derrick said.

She threw him a grateful glance over her shoulder. "Thank you."

He grinned, the wind ruffling his dark hair as he stepped down a rung. "Just don't be such a fool again. That's all the thanks I need."

She followed him, trying to focus on his voice. "Do you climb the rigging often?"

"Once in a while. It's good to keep your head clear." He paused and looked out to sea, the bluish highlights glinting in his black hair. "You never appreciate the sea until you've seen it from up here."

It was beautiful. Deep blue and seemingly endless, it stretched forever on either side. "Does it frighten you at all?"

"Not anymore. It used to, though."

Catherine tightened her grip. "I don't think I'm going to give the rigging a second chance."

"Good," he said. "I've had enough excitement for this voyage. It's a wonder I don't have heart palpitations."

She giggled at the thought of him, so big and strong, succumbing to heart palpitations. "Your heart is as strong as a horse's."

He glanced at her from beneath his lashes, his blue eyes sparkling with mischief. "My heart is not up for discussion."

But why not? The thought surprised her and she had to swallow the retort to keep from saying it aloud. "This is taking a long time. Isn't there a quicker way down?"

He chuckled. "You'll find a quicker way if you don't

move your foot to the left. You're near the edge of that spar."

Catherine obediently shifted to the left, then waited for Derrick to move to the line below.

He reached his place, then glanced up at her. "How is Lucas? I didn't get a chance to check on him this morning."

She clutched the lines and reached below with her toe to find the next line. After a tense moment, she felt it with her foot. "Lucas is much better. He ate some broth and complained it was too salty."

"Sounds as if he'll be up in no time."

"With a little more rest, I think he'll be fine." She stopped for a moment, then said in a solemn voice, "He was very lucky."

"We all were."

Though he'd told her not to, she glanced down at him and caught the gleam of his blue gaze. He had the most beautiful eyes—the bright blue of a winter sky, surrounded by thick lashes. Catherine looked enviously at his lashes—it didn't seem fair for a man to have such lovely lashes.

"How's George taking to life at sea?"

George? Oh yes, her dog. "Little has a fondness for him and feeds him more than he should."

"I thought he looked a little heavier the last time I saw you walking him on deck."

Catherine started to tell Derrick how George had won

over the crew, but as she looked down, she realized they were within a few yards of the deck. Derrick reached it first, then raised his arms and plucked her from the rigging.

"There ye are!" Peters said cheerfully. "Did ye like climbin' the riggin's?"

"It was lovely," Catherine said, her arms about Derrick's neck. She wondered why he didn't release her, but he seemed to have forgotten that he was holding her. What was even more strange was that the crew didn't seem to think anything of it either. Several crewmen offered their congratulations on her feat, while others just grinned happily.

Finally, Catherine looked up at Derrick. "I think you can put me down now."

"Where are your shoes?"

She pointed to a barrel by the mizzenmast, and he carried her to it and set her down. "We've still repairs to make, so be sure you've shoes on until we're done. I don't want you to find a stray nail the hard way."

"Aye, aye, Cap'n," she responded, trying hard not to think about how much she had liked having his arms about her.

He grinned down at her. "I need to check our course. Do you think you can keep out of trouble until then?"

She yanked one of her boots on. "I'll try."

"Good." He reached out and tilted her chin up for a

moment, then let his hand drop. "See that you do."

He was so dear, helping her from the rigging. And for assisting her to find Royce. Catherine didn't think she could ever repay him. "Derrick, I—" She searched for the words.

He raised his brows. "You?" he prompted.

She took a deep breath and plunged forward. "I—I know you're risking a lot to help me, but I want you to know that whatever this journey costs, Royce will gladly pay you."

Derrick's brows lowered. "I am a St. John, Catherine. I do not sell my friendship."

Heat flooded Catherine's face. "Derrick, I didn't mean to suggest that you could be bought. I was just saying that my brother—"

"Would *pay* me for helping you reach Savannah. I heard what you said, Catherine. And I want no part of it."

"You can't expect me to just let you do this for me for nothing!" she exploded, frustrated that he didn't understand how much she owed him. She tried to think of a better way to say it, but it was too late. He was already gone, stalking across the deck, outrage evident in every line of his body.

Catherine sighed and pulled on her other boot. Darn Derrick St. John. It would be hours before he was fit to speak to; he had more pride than any ten men she knew.

And that was just one of the things she both loved and hated about him. "Men," she said with a shake of her head. "Who could ever hope to understand them?" Heart heavy, she hopped off the barrel and went to see Lucas.

CHAPTER TWELVE

The winds favored the *Sea Princess* and they finally reached Savannah. Catherine was surprised by how beautiful it was. Situated at the mouth of a sparkling river, the town was small and quaint. Still, it showed signs of rapid growth—the docks bustled with activity and several large ships were moored, loading and unloading goods.

Many of the Southern plantations were beginning to use this port to ship their goods. Even now, bags of rice and barrels of pecans were stacked neatly alongside the quay. The shops and taverns that lined the cobbled stoned roadway were clean and large. Most harbor towns were suffering because of the war, but Savannah seemed determined to ignore the threat of the British ships patrolling the deeper Atlantic waters.

Catherine tried to still her hammering heart as she looked at the mixture of buildings before her. Somewhere in there her brother was waiting—perhaps hungry, frightened, or injured. If she closed her eyes, she could almost feel his presence. *Be patient, Royce. I'm coming.*

She took a steadying breath. If Royce was injured—the thought made her feel ill and she allowed Poole to distract her with an elaborate show of tying a knot in a piece of rope using only his teeth. It had been this way all day—the crew were well aware of her brother's situation and they knew the moment of truth was at hand. Leaning heavily on a pair of makeshift crutches, Poole had appointed himself her guardian. He stayed by Catherine's side, attempting to amuse her with a string of tales and tricks.

Catherine tried to pay attention, but it was difficult. The bos'n's mate seemed to understand, for when she didn't hear his banter or respond to a joke or question, he would just change the subject.

After a while, Lucas joined them. He was up and about more each day now. Though still pale, he was doing better, his appetite much improved.

Lucas immediately got into the spirit of things and began to show Catherine all manner of complicated ropes with fancy names like "monkey's paw" and "midshipman's hitch."

From the corner of her eye, Catherine caught sight of Derrick as he strode across the deck. The wind lifted his black hair and pulled on his white shirt. She turned away, determined he wouldn't catch her watching him, though that was all she had done since their argument the day before. Catherine supposed it was good that they hadn't tried to talk more. She seemed to make things worse every time she opened her mouth.

"There goes the cap'n," Bransom said, ambling up to watch Lucas tie a bowline. "I hope he's not making a mistake."

"Where's the captain going?" Catherine asked.

Bransom shrugged. "I dunno, but he was awful particular about what we was to do if he was late returnin'. Almost as if he didn't expect to make it back at all."

Lucas nodded. "I polished his boots, twice. And this morning he had Peters brush out his good coat."

A wave of cold certainty clutched Catherine's heart. "I hope he's not going to—" She bit back the words. He wouldn't *dare* go to the meeting without her. *Or would he?*

Catherine hopped off the barrel she'd been sitting on. "I think I'll have a word with the captain." Or she would if he would stop avoiding her since their blowup.

"At least see if ye can convince him to take me wif him," Thompson called after her. "He needs someone to watch his back."

And that someone would be her, Catherine decided. It was just like Derrick to plan on leaving her behind. He was overly concerned about her safety—worse even than Royce had been. She marched across the deck and up the short ladder to where Derrick stood, talking with Smythe while Peters helped him shrug into his blue coat.

Catherine hesitated for an instant. Dressed in the blue coat faced with white trim and silver buttons, his white shirt neatly tucked in, a knotted tie at his throat and his black boots polished to a high sheen, he looked hearstoppingly handsome. Handsome *and* commanding.

Derrick caught sight of her and frowned. "I was just going to send for you. I need the gold."

Of course he did. And she needed her brother back. "I'll fetch it," she said as sweetly as her clenched teeth would allow. "It will only take me a few moments to change."

His expression darkened. "You don't need to change. You aren't going with me."

Smythe clucked his tongue and shook his head, mumbling about young men who didn't know the strength of a woman's determination.

Catherine ignored Smythe, her gaze locked on Derrick. "Pardon me, but did you say I wasn't going ashore?"

"That's exactly what I said and you know it. I am going to deliver the ransom. Please don't argue. Just get the gold. I know we aren't due to pay the ransom for another two days, but perhaps we can get this over with sooner."

"You would go without me?"

"Yes," he said in a grimly certain voice.

Smythe looked from one to the other and scratched his ear. "Pardon me, Cap'n, but Miss Markham has gone through a lot of trouble to find her brother. Don't ye think ye should—"

"Is this any of your business?" Derrick said, an awful frown on his face.

The first mate shuffled his feet. "No, not particularly.

However, I do think it be me duty to point out—"

"Have the deck scrubbed while I'm away."

Smythe sighed and sent Catherine an apologetic look. "Sorry, miss. No matter what, he is the cap'n."

"He's not *my* captain."

Smythe appeared impressed at that bit of logic. "No, he's not." Derrick's scowl seemed to reach him at that moment and the first mate turned a bright red, then scurried off, calling for the men to gather buckets as he went.

"Derrick, you cannot go ashore without me," Catherine said. "Not without the gold, you won't."

"Then it's a good thing I know where the gold is, isn't it? I wanted to be polite, but—" He shrugged and then turned on his heel.

Catherine scrambled to make it to the ladder first. She was but two paces in front of him when she planted herself on the closest step. "You wait just one minute, Derrick St. John! I didn't come all this way just to watch you make a hero of yourself."

"I'm not making a hero of myself," he growled, raking a hand through his hair. "Damn it, Catherine! Royce would have me keelhauled for putting you in danger. Whatever happens, I won't have you hurt."

"May I remind you that we are talking about *my* brother? Not yours."

"Catherine, just listen to reason—"

"I have to be there for him. What if he is hurt? He will need me."

Derrick frowned. "Look, I don't want to argue. But I can't let you risk yourself in such a way—"

"Then I'll go without you."

"You wouldn't dare."

"Try me."

"Catherine—" He glared down at her, his jaw tight with frustration. "You are a spoiled brat, far too used to getting your own way."

"And you are an insufferable beast who thinks you can order everyone about as if they were members of your crew. I have news for you, Captain Derrick St. John. I am *not* a member of your crew."

His gaze went to her pants. "You look like one."

"A few minutes and I'll be more presentable."

He hesitated, then sighed. "You are incorrigible."

"Among other things." She lifted a brow. "Well?"

"I suppose I have no choice." He shot her a hard glance. "I'll give you five minutes and no more."

"Done!" Before he could change his mind, she turned and scurried to the cabin. Once there, she yanked her clothing from the trunk, thinking wistfully of the maid who had kept all of her gowns so neatly pressed at High Hill. Oh well, she would just be a bit wrinkled. There was nothing wrong with that.

Though she hurried, it took her longer than five minutes to get ready, mainly because of the difficulties she had in tightening her corset without anyone's help. The last thing she did before venturing up on deck was to comb out her hair and twist it on top of her head in a simple knot. She secured it with the few pins she had, wishing she had a mirror to check the results. Then, the bag of gold in her pocket, she opened the door and hurried to the deck.

She was met with a wall of silence. Lucas shook his head. "Ye look beautiful, miss. Jus' like an angel."

Everyone seemed appreciative of her appearance except, of course, Derrick. He raked a cold look over her, then said, "Do you have the gold?"

She nodded and he led the way down the gangplank. He didn't speak as they walked and Catherine took note of the crowded town. Wagons rolled up and down the cobbled street, vendors hawked their wares on the corner. "Royce always said I would like this town."

He flicked a glance at her. "Did he ever take you on his travels?"

"Never. I kept asking, of course, and he'd always promise to take me next time, but somehow that never happened."

"That's his loss. You are a superb traveler."

Catherine was so surprised by the compliment that she almost stumbled. "Do you think so?"

"I know it." Derrick looked about him as if noticing the town for the first time. "I was here a year ago. It's grown."

"I suppose everything grows up after a while, even towns."

"Everything except exasperating girls who are determined to run straight into harm's way."

"I'll have you know that I intend to be helpful." She patted her skirts where they hid her pocket. "I even brought a gun."

He stopped. "You brought a *what?*"

"A gun. Just in case something goes wrong. No one would expect me to have a pistol."

"Where did you get it?"

"Smythe."

"I'm going to have a word with that man when we return. He is far too involved in my affairs."

"Ah, but this time he was busy in *my* affairs and I am quite grateful for it. Therefore you have no reason whatsoever to be upset with the poor man."

Derrick closed his eyes for a moment. "Has anyone ever told you how annoying you are?"

"Royce. A hundred times, at least."

"It wasn't enough," Derrick said sourly, though his eyes glinted with reluctant amusement.

"I think I should be insulted by that."

He turned into an alley beside a dark, dingy tavern and grinned down at her. "I haven't begun to insult you. But soon. Soon."

He was trying to distract her, and for that she couldn't

help but be thankful. Every step led them deeper and deeper into the alleyway where dark shadows cast a cold pall.

She managed a smile. "I hope we don't have to walk far—" She came to a halt. Hanging from an iron rod was a wooden sign. *The Red Rooster Inn* was painted on it in faded red. Catherine's chest tightened and she had to fight the desire to run ahead. Royce was so close—she could feel it. "This is it," she said, noting the small group of men who slouched on a bench outside the tavern, as if waiting for it to open.

Derrick nodded, his face somber. "Yes, it is."

Catherine inspected what she could see of the building. The place looked deserted. The door hung crookedly, the windows stared out, cracked and, in some places, missing, and the chimney leaned heavily to one side as if a strong wind would send it toppling over.

Derrick straightened his shoulders. "Catherine, listen to me. The people who took Royce will want to see the gold, and things could get out of hand. That's why I wanted you to stay behind."

"I don't understand."

"If by some mischance, something has happened to Royce, they may try to take the gold by force." He looked down at her, his expression serious, his blue gaze intent. "If anything happens, promise me you will run."

"And leave you? That would be cowardly! I couldn't—"

"Catherine, if you don't promise me this one thing, I will not allow you to step foot inside that tavern. I've faced worse than this and survived, but if I have to worry about you . . . Just say that you will run and won't look back."

"But Derrick, what if—"

"There are no what-ifs. You must promise." He grasped her hands and pulled her around to face him. "Now."

Catherine didn't want to promise him anything. But his mouth was set in a firm line and the years of commanding his own ship had given him an implacable sense of command. Sighing with impatience, she nodded. "I promise to run if there is trouble. Just help Royce. Please, Derrick."

His hands tightened over hers. "We'll get him back, Catherine. I promise."

For some reason, the quiet words resonated deep in her heart. Whatever happened, they were together. There was a strange comfort in the thought. The wind blew down the alley and lifted a strand of her hair and blew it across her face. She pulled her hand free and tucked the strand behind her ear.

As she did so, she caught the gaze of one of the men who lounged outside the doorway of the tavern. He was a short man, shorter than Catherine by a good two inches. His reddish hair hung to his thin shoulders, his angular face marred by pockmarks. Catherine had to repress a shudder at the uneasy feeling that immediately invaded her.

Derrick frowned. "Are you cold?"

"No, I—" She what? Was afraid at just the sight of a common sailor? She managed a smile. "Nothing. Shall we go in?"

"Of course." Derrick took her hand and proceeded to the tavern.

Just as he reached the door, the pockmarked man stood up. "Aye, there," he said, his furtive gaze taking in both Derrick and Catherine. "The Red Rooster is not open."

From where she stood, Catherine could hear the sound of tankards slapping wooden tables, and the murmur of voices. "It sounds open," she said.

"Well, it ain't," the man sneered. The two men with him suddenly stood. "Perhaps ye'd best return from whence ye came."

"No," Derrick said, his jaw taut. "We've business here."

"The only business ye have is with me."

Catherine heard a movement behind her, and she knew without looking that more men had arrived in the shadowy alleyway. She tried to swallow. "Look, I don't know what you want, but we're here to meet with someone about—"

"Yer brother?" The man smiled, revealing a row of brown and broken teeth. "Mayhap ye've already come to the right place."

"But the missive said to ask the owner for instructions. Is that you?"

The pock-faced man's grin didn't diminish a bit. "Things have changed."

"I don't like this," Derrick said.

"Neither do I," Catherine agreed. She looked at their captors. "What do you want?"

The man's smile widened. "There's someone who wants to have a word with ye."

"And if I don't wish to speak with this someone?"

"Oh, ye'll speak to him. The question is whether ye'll do it standin' or tied up like a rat."

Derrick's hand closed over Catherine's arm. "Remember your promise," he whispered to her behind clenched teeth.

Catherine bit back a sharp answer. It was ludicrous to think that she'd run like a coward just because Derrick had made her promise. On the other hand, if it looked as if she might be able to escape and go for help . . . the thought took hold. Perhaps that was just what she should do.

Another strand of her hair loosened and she lifted her hand to push it back, the gesture turning her head slightly as she did so. It was then that she caught a reflection in a broken window of the two men who had emerged from the shadows of the alley to stand behind them. Both men held pistols, the barrels pointed at Derrick's back.

Oblivious to the danger, Derrick eyed the pockmarked man with disgust. "What do you want?"

Catherine grasped his arm, pressing her fingernails

into his skin. He glanced down at her and she nodded to the window. His gaze followed hers, and a moment later, he bit back a curse.

The leader watched the exchange with interest. "Aye, matey. Ye're outnumbered, ye are. So best ye save yerself an' the lady a bit o' heartbreak an' come along nice an' quiet."

Catherine sighed. "Come on, Derrick. We have no choice." She could see that he wanted to argue, but couldn't. After a tense moment, he nodded.

The pockmarked man smirked. "Don't ye worry none, laddie. We won't be goin' far. Ye'll see what's goin' to happen to ye soon enough." With that, the man turned and led them farther down the alleyway. Catherine and Derrick had no choice but to follow, aware of the guns trained on their backs.

CHAPTER THIRTEEN

The red-haired man led the way down the dirty alley and through a confusing assortment of narrow streets and passageways. Finally, they stopped before a rickety building that appeared as if a puff of wind could blow it down.

Someone must have been watching for them, for the door opened as soon as they stepped onto the crooked steps leading to the front door. The interior of the house was as grim as the outside. Every piece of furniture was broken or bent, the walls, floors, and ceiling an oppressive gray, and the air damp and fetid.

Derrick cursed his weakness in bringing Catherine. Not that she'd given him a choice—she would have come no matter what, with or without him.

The four men led them up a narrow set of stairs and down a dark hallway that smelled strongly of mold. At the farthest door, the red-haired man knocked with a complicated series of coded beats. The door opened and he stood aside, motioning Derrick and Catherine into the room.

The tiny room was airless and even darker than the hall, only one lantern offering any light. All of the windows were shuttered and locked. Derrick strained to see in the darkness.

"Ah, Captain St. John and the lovely *Mademoiselle* Markham," said someone from the darkest corner. The man's voice was strangely cultured, a faint French accent smoothing the words. "Welcome to my humble abode. Pray come in and be seated. Oh, and put the money on the table, if you please."

Derrick's eyes adjusted to the light and he could make out the man who addressed them. He was shabbily if elegantly dressed, his black hair shimmering in the dim light, his black eyes cold and deadly. A wave of recognition froze Derrick's thoughts. It was DeGardineau, the man whose lies had sealed the fate of Derrick's father.

A loud roar filled Derrick's ears and he bolted forward, his hands fisted. *Click.* A gun was cocked. Even in his frenzied state, Derrick caught himself. Catherine was here. He had to hold his temper for her, if not for himself.

"Well, well, well. Captain St. John," DeGardineau said, stepping out of the shadows. "We finally meet."

Derrick longed to plant his fist in the man's smiling face, but now was not the time. The thought burned in his stomach like acid.

Catherine looked from DeGardineau to Derrick and then back again. "Who are you?"

The Frenchman bowed with a flourish. "Jean Paul

DeGardineau. At your service, *mademoiselle.*"

"And what business have you with us?" Catherine asked.

Through a haze of fury, Derrick felt a tug of pride. She had to know, just as he did, that the men in this room meant to harm them. But Catherine showed no fear. She stood tall and proud, her chin in the air, her lips pressed into a thin line with disgust for the men who held her prisoner.

Derrick could see that her manner impressed the men, even DeGardineau.

The man chuckled a little now. "What business indeed?" He rested a hand on his hip, the gesture pulling his coat back to reveal the cold bone handle of a wicked-looking knife. "I know why you are here."

Catherine paled at the sight of the knife. "You have my brother—"

"Do I? Now you are making assumptions. *Never* assume anything."

A look of confusion flickered across her face. "If you don't have Royce, then why did you bring us here?"

Derrick gave a short laugh. "The money, Catherine. That's all they want."

DeGardineau smiled, his teeth white. "Very good, St. John! You are here to deliver a quantity of gold and so here I am."

"No. I cannot give it to you," Catherine said. "It would mean my brother's life."

The Frenchman nodded sadly. "Ah, the choices one must sometimes make. Your brother's life . . ." He pulled the knife from his belt and regarded the lantern light. "Or yours. Which will it be?"

"Catherine," Derrick said, aware of a desperate tightness in his chest. "Give them the money. We have no choice."

"Derrick, I can't. Royce—"

"Will die if you are not there to meet the people who captured him."

"But the gold—"

"We can deal with that later."

"Ah," DeGardineau said with evident approval. "You are a man of sense. I should dislike you intensely, but I find I cannot."

"DeGardineau, take the money and leave," Derrick said, his jaw aching with the effort he was making not to toss caution to the wind and fly at the man he hated.

"Oh, I will take the money." The Frenchman laughed softly. "Have no fear on that score."

Catherine clamped her mouth shut, but she knew that Derrick had spoken the truth. She reached into her pocket and slowly pulled out the sack.

"Put it on the table," the Frenchman ordered.

Catherine hefted it in her hand, then reached toward

the table, catching Derrick's gaze briefly. Something flickered there—a message of some sort. She paused, her mind whirling. Then she reached out with the bag of gold as if to place it on the table.

At the last minute, she tossed the bag to Derrick. *"Run!"*

Derrick wrapped his fingers tightly over the pouch and planted his fist in the face of the nearest man. The weight of the gold made his punch all the more lethal and the man dropped to the floor like an anchor. A large greasy man with arms like ham hocks strode forward. Derrick drew back as if to punch the man, but kicked him instead. The man staggered back and Derrick went after him.

"*Hold, St. John!* I have the girl."

Derrick froze. The red-haired man held Catherine, his knife glittering against her white skin.

He couldn't swallow, couldn't breathe. All he could do was stare at the knife. The weight of the gold in his hand seemed to increase. Inside the leather bag was enough gold to purchase either Royce's life or Catherine's, but not both.

There was no choice. Derrick dropped the bag on the table with a thud.

"No!" Catherine gasped.

He raised his gaze to hers, steeling himself for her

sorrow. "Royce would expect me to guard your safety over his own. We have to give them the gold."

"A difficult choice," DeGardineau declared sardonically. He took the bag and pulled the cord from the opening, then poured the coins onto the table. The gold drew the light from the lantern, swelling the room with a yellow glow.

"Count it." DeGardineau nodded to one of the dirty men who were even now getting to their feet. One man staggered to the table, wiping blood from his nose. His beefy face lit up when he saw the coins. Laboriously, he began sorting the coins into stacks.

The Frenchman waved his gun. "Tie St. John to the chair."

Another henchman lurched forward and pushed Derrick into a chair. The man lashed Derrick's arms so tightly that the cord bit into his skin. But the pain was nothing compared to the fear that the knife at Catherine's throat sent through him.

It was all Derrick could do to speak in a calm voice. He shot a hard stare at the Frenchman. "If she is harmed, I will kill you. I already owe you that much as it is."

DeGardineau grinned, his teeth glinting in the lamplight. "It is unfortunate that you won't be alive to enact any thrilling tales of vengeance." He skulked to Catherine's side. Derrick's heart hammered in his chest as he watched the Frenchman place a dirty hand on her chin. "I've always had a soft heart for a pretty face." He lifted the lantern so that the light flickered over her.

Derrick could see the tearstains on her pale cheeks, anguish in her green eyes at the thought of losing the gold that was to purchase Royce's freedom. His heart ached. "Leave her be."

The Frenchman's attention returned to Derrick. "Frightened for her, are you? You should be. Such a tasty morsel wouldn't last long if I were to give her to my men."

"You wouldn't dare," Derrick ground out.

DeGardineau held the lantern a bit higher, tracing a dirty finger down her cheek. "You may have the right of it. 'Twould be foolishness to waste such a pretty one." His black gaze shifted to Derrick, though he remained at Catherine's side. "But you . . . you're expendable."

Catherine jerked away. "And you, sir, are a coward!"

The Frenchman's smile disappeared. He sank his hand into Catherine's hair, jerked her head back, and leaned down until his face was but inches from hers. "I am *not* a coward, *mademoiselle*. You'd do well to remember that."

Derrick fastened the man with a hard look. "You have your money. Now leave."

The Frenchman turned to him. "Always in charge, aren't you? Always telling others what to do. You are very like your father."

"Don't talk to me about my father. You have said

more than enough as it is."

"Ah, yes. The little inquest. I did have a lot to say then, didn't I?"

"All of it false."

"Not all of it. He was a fine captain. A bit shortsighted, but a fine captain for all that."

"He was a good man, a fearless captain and he would *never* have turned his back on the colonies."

DeGardineau shrugged. "He was noble; I'll give you that. But alas, like all of us, he was flawed."

"Never."

"Spoken like a devoted son. But he did have a failing—pride. He didn't know an opportunity even when 'twas pointed out to him."

"He believed hard work was the way to success. Which you would know if you had been truly close to him."

The man's smile darkened. "I was as close to him as I wished to be. Closer than he wished, at the end."

A chill struck Derrick's chest. "What do you mean 'at the end'?"

The man counting the money turned the last coin into a neat pile. "Fifty gold pieces. Just as ye'd been told."

Derrick's gaze narrowed. "You knew how many gold pieces we carried and you knew where we were to deliver them. Not many people have that information."

Catherine made a convulsive movement, and Derrick

realized she thought the same thing he did—only her uncle had that information from the ransom note.

The Frenchman chuckled. "You are indeed an intelligent man, St. John, perhaps even more so than your father." The man's gaze rested on Catherine. "I admire your courage, *mademoiselle*. You have more than your uncle. He is a real coward, that one. You can almost smell it on him."

Catherine closed her eyes for a moment. "I never knew he hated me so much."

DeGardineau shook his head regretfully. "Men like Elliot Markham do not hate. They don't have the capacity. Those with great hatred in their hearts also have room for great love."

"Such poetry." Derrick sneered. "And all from a petty thief. Who would believe it?"

"I may be a thief, but I am never petty. I am DeGardineau, the greatest thief in the world."

Derrick leaned forward. "When I get out of here, you are a dead man, DeGardineau."

"Indeed? May I point out that you are greatly outnumbered."

"I've been outnumbered before and won my way free."

"You sound more and more like your father."

"Leave my father out of this. You aren't even fit to mention his name."

DeGardineau looked amused. "He always said he was

raising you to be a gentleman. But look at you now. All muddied and beaten. Tsk, tsk."

"I'm not beaten."

"Not yet," the man said with a cold grin. "But you will be soon." He glanced at the burly guards who stood at either side of Derrick and nodded. "Kill him. And when you're finished, toss his body into the water."

"And the girl?" one of the men growled.

DeGardineau's black gaze slid over Catherine. "It is a waste, I know, but I have made an agreement. Kill her, too."

"You are despicable!" Catherine said hotly. "Derrick is twice the man you are."

DeGardineau leaned closer to Catherine, who closed her eyes and turned away. "A lovely young thing, she is. Perhaps I've been a bit hasty. I should keep her for myself—"

Derrick erupted, launching himself across the table, chair and all. His body connected with DeGardineau with a solid thud. The man cried out and fell back against the wall as the guards grabbed Derrick.

Hands cupped over his face, blood seeping down his cheek, DeGardineau staggered to his feet. "Damn you, St. John! You are a dead man!"

Derrick struggled against the guards, but they held him securely.

DeGardineau stumbled to the table and glared down at

Derrick, his face twisted with hate. "I'll see you end up like your father, twenty fathoms deep, branded a worthless traitor!"

"My father was no traitor."

"That's not what I saw." DeGardineau sneered. "He was a traitor, if not to his colors, then to us, his men."

"How so?" Here at last, was the truth. "How was he a traitor?"

"We were facing a battle we could not win. The British outmanned us, their ship was larger and had more cannon. All we had to do was surrender. They'd have spared most of us. But your father—" DeGardineau's face turned a deep red, his mouth twisted in an angry sneer.

"My father refused their terms," Derrick said slowly, in wonder. He could see it all now—the battle had turned for the worse, his father's ship outclassed by the larger, more heavily armed vessel. It must have been painfully obvious to his father and the crew, too. "You . . . the crew . . . you turned on him. You were the ones to change the flag, not my father."

"We wanted to survive, and he, dripping with talk about glory and honor, refused to give us even that chance." DeGardineau shook his head bitterly. "We had no choice but to kill him."

"The entire crew was with you?"

"There were one or two who refused to assist us. We

took care of them when we dealt with your father."

Derrick's chest ached with pain at the thought. Hot rage roared in his ears. "Damn you, DeGardineau. How could you—"

"How could I?" The man asked, his voice rising with each word. "How could I? Let me tell you something, you blasted fool! What else could I, or anyone else on that ship do? He gave us no choice—it was surrender or die. So we chose death, only not our own."

"You killed him, then joined those filthy Brits."

"We made good money for that little trick. After all, your father's ship was well known in those waters. We'd sail up to an American ship, wait until we were almost alongside her and then *bam!* We'd attack." DeGardineau smiled. "It was a grand adventure. And when it lost its flavor, we went home and told the authorities that your father had made the decisions. That we had argued against it, but that he was fanatical. They believed it and we were free of any charges of wrongdoing."

"And given commendations of bravery for finally facing him down."

"That was a nice addition to the story, was it not? We were welcomed home as heroes. And your father . . . well, he was dead. What did it matter if his name was covered with dishonor?"

"It matters to me, his son."

"You? You have no honor, St. John. You see, I know all about you." He stood and gestured to one of his men, who came forward and scooped the gold back into the bag.

Derrick clenched his hands into fists. He didn't dare look at Catherine. He couldn't bear to see the disgust and horror on her face. "I have changed, DeGardineau."

"Have you, indeed? It's a pity that I do not care, one way or the other." He took the pouch of gold and tucked it into his pocket, then nodded to the thin, red-haired man. "Come, Marcel. Let's leave the others to their duties. I have wasted enough time here."

"Wait," Catherine said. "Where is my brother?"

DeGardineau halted for a moment by the door and smoothed his coat. "That is a good question, my pretty. But even if I had the answer . . . what good would it do you now?" With a jaunty tip of his hat, he left.

There was a tense silence as the door closed. They listened as the footsteps faded into silence.

The man holding Catherine tightened his grip until she could barely breathe. How was she going to get out of this one, she wondered hopelessly.

Snap! Derrick bolted from his chair and Catherine realized that he'd been pressing steadily against the ropes that held him captive, and the chair had finally broken. He snatched up the lantern and slammed it into the face of the man beside him, who stumbled backward with a cry and fell to the floor in a motionless heap. The man holding Catherine shoved her to one side and yanked a knife from his belt.

"Catherine, run!" Derrick shouted, forcing himself not to think of Catherine's pale face. He launched himself on the two guards, knocking them to the floor. As soon as he hit the floor, he rolled to his feet and found himself facing two more furious men. All Derrick could hope was that he'd given Catherine time to escape.

The man closest held a wicked knife. He showed his teeth in a menacing fashion and flashed the blade. One other guard regained his footing and joined him, pulling a gun from his belt and pointing it at Derrick.

He was lost. But he'd be damned if he would go down without a fight. Gathering himself, he prepared to launch himself again on the nearest burly guard.

But before he could act, a shot rang out. Wood splintered from the wall beside the fat guard's head. He went pale, his gaze fastened on the doorway.

Catherine's voice came, calm and clear. "If you so much as move an inch, I will put a bullet between your eyes."

The other guard whirled, his own gun lifting, but Catherine was quicker. She squeezed the trigger again and the guard's gun flew in the air. He cried out, clutching his bloodied hand. He groaned and sank to the floor.

Derrick gave a relieved sigh. "I owe Smythe my thanks for giving you that gun."

Catherine managed a smile. "He deserves more than that."

"I think ye've forgotten one thing," the other guard said. A slow, malevolent grin spread over the man's broad face. "That'd be yer last bullet. And yer last hope of getting' out o' here alive."

"Not quite," Derrick said. He drew back his fist and hit the man so hard, the guard reeled back and slammed into the wall, then slid to a motionless heap on the floor.

Derrick took the rope from where he'd been bound and tied all of the men securely. Then he turned to Catherine. She stood a little ways away, leaning against the door, her hands still clenched about the pistol.

He crossed to her and gently loosened her fingers from the gun and put it on the table. Then he put an arm about her shoulders and pulled her against him. She fit perfectly, her head reaching his chin, the warm lemony smell of her hair tickling his nose. It felt so good, so *right* to stand with her in his arms.

But DeGardineau had all but revealed Derrick's past. Catherine had to know what he'd been. He pulled away, dropping his arms to his sides. She must hate him, even now. The thought hurt with all the pain of a fresh wound.

Derrick cleared his throat. "We should go."

"I know," she whispered, raising her gaze to his. "Derrick, I—"

The door flew open and Smythe burst in, followed quickly by Jacobs. Smythe glanced around, taking in the fallen men with a practiced eye. "We missed all the fun." He turned to Jacobs. "Ye fool. I *tol'* ye the cap'n didn't need us to help him."

Jacobs poked at one of the prone men with the toe of his boot. "He'll need our help if'n he's wanting someone to carry these sorry carcasses back to the ship. What are we to do wif' 'em?"

"Take them on board and put them in the brig." Derrick held out his hand to Catherine. "Let's go back, Catherine. Back to the *Sea Princess*."

She looked at his hand, but made no move to take it. "But what about my brother? Without the money, he is as good as dead."

"We have until tomorrow. We'll think of something."

Her gaze drifted over him, resting on his eyes, his mouth. He half expected her to step away from him, to tell him she never wanted to see him again. But to his surprise, she lifted her hand and rested it on his cheek. "You are right. Together, we will save Royce."

Derrick's heart lightened. Was it possible that she hadn't understood DeGardineau's utterance about Derrick's past?

Perhaps the tension of the moment had forced it from her mind.

Whatever the reason, Derrick was grateful. He covered her hand with his and smiled down at her. "Together, then." With that, he led her outside into the sunshine.

CHAPTER FOURTEEN

Catherine stood on the deck of the *Sea Princess*, George a pool of warm fur on her feet. The night sky shone brightly, no clouds hiding the twinkle of the stars above. The waves lapped peacefully against the hull, rocking the ship against the dock with a gentle thumping. And somewhere nearby, Royce was waiting, perhaps despairing that no one was coming to rescue him.

She and Derrick had but one thing in their favor—the kidnappers didn't know that the gold was lost. It was the one thing keeping Royce alive. But as soon as they met and the kidnappers asked for the gold . . .

Catherine tilted her face to the sky and said a fervent prayer. *Please let Royce be safe.*

"It's a lovely night, isn't it?" came a deep voice.

Catherine turned to find Derrick behind her. He'd just come from a bath, for his hair was still damp, curling against his neck, his shirt clinging to his damp skin. Catherine had a bath hours earlier in an attempt to wash away some of the despair that cloaked her ever since the thieves had stolen the gold. Just having Derrick standing here with her made her believe that perhaps things would turn out right.

Catherine glanced up at the rigging swaying overhead and remembered how he'd helped her climb down when she'd gotten stuck. "I think I know why you love this ship." She put her hands on the railing and leaned back, letting the cold breeze lift her hair and riffle through her skirts. "She makes you feel free."

"Yes, she does." Derrick closed the space between them to stand beside Catherine, nudging George with one foot. "Move, mutt."

George wagged his tail but didn't budge.

"George," Catherine said. "You heard him. Now move."

The dog rolled onto his back, asking for a tummy rub.

Catherine gave a sigh of exasperation before she bent and scratched him. "There. Now go and lie somewhere else." This time she shoved him.

He scrambled to his feet, panting so hard it looked as if he had a grin on his furry face. He wagged his tail, then walked a few feet away and dropped into his usual sleeping position.

Derrick shook his head. "Does he ever do what you say?"

"Never. When he was a pup, I kept thinking he'd do better when he got older. Well, he's older now, and he's just as bad as he was then."

They looked at the dog for a moment and Catherine

tried desperately to think of something more to say. She could feel the tension in the air, as if Derrick was as nervous as she.

Derrick looked up at the swaying masts, his shoulder brushing hers. "It's strange how you grow to love a place or a thing. The *Sea Princess* is not just a ship. She's my home."

Catherine glanced at him curiously, noticing the way his lashes cast shadows over his cheeks. "Do you want to live your entire life on board ship?"

"I . . . don't know. Perhaps I do want a house. A family." He smiled down at her. "What about you?"

"I don't know. It's strange, but I always thought you wanted this. . . ." She gestured to the ship. "To live free and unfettered."

"I've been free and unfettered," he said lightly. "While it can be exhilarating, it can also be lonely."

"Lonely? With the crew about?" Catherine couldn't imagine being lonely on ship.

"When you are captain, you don't have the luxury of making friends with the crew."

That was true. And now that Catherine thought about it, except for Smythe, she never saw Derrick engage in casual conversation with the men. "There's one or two you can talk to that are closer."

"Smythe. He was my father's first mate and should have been with him when . . ." Derrick paused. "Smythe came down with the ague right before the ship was to set sail. I think he's always wondered if things might have been different if he'd been on board."

Catherine knew he spoke of his father's last voyage. She yearned to comfort him, to give him ease in some small way. "I need to thank you."

He seemed to relax then, for he shrugged. "We lost the money, Catherine. I should have known—"

"How could you have guessed that DeGardineau, of all people, would turn up? Neither of us saw it coming. But you've done so much for me. And Royce, too. I don't think anyone else would have helped the way you have."

Derrick's smile was lost in the shadows. He crossed his arms over his chest and said, "You're wrong. You would have done the same for me or anyone else you thought was in trouble."

She would have done all this and more for him, Catherine realized. But all she said was, "Perhaps."

"Catherine, if there is one thing I know, it is to appreciate your true friends. Sometimes they are all you have."

His voice was deep, almost gentle. Catherine placed her hand on his, her heart full. Perhaps it was the tension from the previous day, or the realization that, one way or another, their adventure was about to come to an end. Or perhaps it was just the simple fact that he was standing beside her, his hand warm beneath hers and it felt so *right*. Whatever it was, Catherine heard herself say, "Derrick,

I . . . I care for you. Very, very much."

She held her breath, waiting.

He didn't say anything for a long, long time. Then a sigh broke from him. "Catherine, I care for you, too."

Her heart leaped. But before she could say anything, he continued.

"When I was at my lowest, Royce gave me another chance. In a way, you and Royce are like family now. My family."

Disappointment swept through her. She'd hoped for something more. "I see," she managed to say.

After a moment, she turned away, suddenly anxious to turn the topic. "Once we have Royce back, we need to find DeGardineau. We have to clear your father's name."

"I will find him. I will not rest until I do. I sent out as many men as I could spare to scour the coast in both directions."

"He is a scoundrel."

"And worse. But never fear, I will find him," Derrick repeated. "And he will undo the harm he has caused."

"Why is it so important to you? Your father is gone now; it can't hurt him."

"Because it hurts my mother. She doesn't deserve to bear more pain than she already has."

Catherine nodded mutely. Derrick would pursue DeGardineau even if it meant endangering his own safety. For most of her life, she'd had a vague belief that somehow, good people always won. It had been a naïve belief, she could see that now. She was beginning to understand that sometimes it wasn't who was right and who was wrong, but who was willing to sacrifice the most.

It was possible that they would not be able to rescue Royce. It was also possible that Derrick would pursue DeGardineau and never return. Tears slowly welled in her eyes.

"Catherine," Derrick said quietly.

She tried to speak. Tried to tell him all the thoughts that jumbled inside and caused her such pain, but the words wouldn't come. Without another word, he enfolded her in his arms and held her close. His warmth seeped through his fine linen shirt and she was surrounded by his strength and his wonderful scent.

Catherine sighed, resting her head against his shoulder. The night wind blew through her, but Catherine didn't feel it. Derrick might not care for her the way she cared for him, but at least they were together now. The thought didn't make her feel better.

"Derrick, what are we going to do about Royce?" she finally asked. "We don't have the gold."

"Shhh," Derrick said. He rubbed his chin against her hair. "We'll find a way, Catherine. Just give me some time."

"We may only have until tomorrow."

"That's all I need." He tilted her face to his, so he could see into her eyes. "Do you trust me, Catherine?"

He waited . . . wondering. She hadn't said a word about his past as a pirate, and he wondered if she'd thought about it. He could see the questions in her eyes. But why would she care what Derrick had once been? He was nothing more than her brother's best friend. That was all.

The truth was harsh, but Derrick was accustomed to harsh truths. He stood with his arms about Catherine. She looked up at him, her eyes wide, her lashes spiked from her tears.

She nodded. "Of course I trust you."

"That's all I ask. Tomorrow we shall return to the Red Rooster. They will still be awaiting payment. Perhaps we can at least see if Royce is alive."

"But—"

"Let me deal with the money. You just be ready in the morning. Catherine, it might be risky."

She nodded. "I know that. But Royce is worth it."

And so was she. He stepped back, his mind racing. He would not let her or Royce down. "It's time you went to bed, Catherine. We have much to do tomorrow."

She nodded, still looking unconvinced. She called George in a soft voice and, when the dog didn't respond, she grabbed him by the collar and tugged him toward the hold. Derrick watched them go, his mind racing. There was one way to get money quickly. It was chancy, but it was all he had.

He turned toward the foredeck where the night watch stood ready. "Poole," he called softly. "I'm going ashore."

Derrick sent for Smythe as soon as the first fingers of light tickled the edge of the horizon. It took him less then two minutes to hand the note to the first mate and explain his errand.

Smythe paled. "Ye can't be serious, Cap'n! The *Sea Princess* is all ye've got."

"I know that," Derrick said. He'd slept but little the previous night, after he'd returned. As he'd lain in the darkness, the ornate clock beside his bunk ticking away each second, he had realized his limited options. But he had no choice if he was to help Catherine and Royce. "Just do it."

Smythe shook his head, all three chins wagging along. "But Cap'n, what if—"

"Do it, Smythe."

The first mate remained where he was. "Surely there's some other way to raise the blunt."

"Such as?" Derrick caught the first mate's worried gaze and managed a smile. "I didn't wish this any more than you, but we've no choice. Deliver the note to a Mr. Jenkins. His house is on Willow Lane by the pier. He'll have something for you to bring me in return."

The first mate rubbed his neck and sighed. "Aye, aye, Cap'n. If ye're certain this is what ye want."

"I'm positive." Derrick softened a little at the crestfallen expression on the first mate's face. "Don't worry, Smythe. All will be well. Bring the packet from Mr. Jenkins to me at the Red Rooster."

"Aye, but I don't trust no money lender, especially not one who makes ye sign yer ship over to him to back yer loan."

"I do not intend to rely on Mr. Jenkins's kindness. I *will* make good on my debt. The ship will not be lost. You have my word on it."

Smythe's face cleared. "Aye aye, Cap'n! If ye say 'tis so, then 'tis so."

Derrick rubbed a hand over his face. It was difficult risking the *Sea Princess*, especially now that she was finally his.

But today's events were more important than a mere ship. He remembered Catherine's face from last night, how haunted she'd looked, and his chest tightened. He prayed that Royce was alive and well.

Smythe carefully tucked the note into his shirt sleeve. "Ye know, 'tis robbery to give only fifty gold pieces against a ship like this. 'Tis a pittance of what she's worth."

"I'm only glad I won't have to pay back more."

A knock sounded on the door. Without waiting for an answer, Lucas stuck his head around the edge. "There's a message fer ye, Cap'n! 'Tis from the Red Rooster." He held out a dirty scrap of paper.

Derrick took it and read it. When he finished, he

placed the note on the table. The torn and dirty paper was unsigned, the ungainly writing more a scrawl than anything else. Derrick frowned. The moment he'd seen DeGardineau and realized the man was somehow connected with Catherine's uncle, Derrick had wondered if he'd found Royce's kidnapper.

He fingered the edge of the letter. But DeGardineau already had the money. Who, then, was holding Royce Markham prisoner?

Derrick looked at Smythe. "You've less than an hour to bring me that gold."

Smythe nodded briskly. "I'll be back in a trice. See if I'm not." He saluted smartly and marched out the door.

Derrick watched him go and then yelled for Lucas. The cabin boy came almost at once. "Go and get Miss Markham. Tell her it's time."

CHAPTER FIFTEEN

"I hope Royce is fine," Catherine said for the fourteenth time as they walked through the busy streets to the Red Rooster. Her eyes were shadowed with worry.

"I'm sure he is," Derrick said soothingly. He glanced down the street. Where was Smythe? He should have returned by now.

Catherine nodded, her movements jerky, uncertain. She was sick with worry and Derrick wished with all his heart he could ease her fears. It was for that reason that he'd allowed her to bring George. The lovable mutt padded along behind them, sniffing the air as if searching out the best locale for his lunch.

Catherine wrung her hands. "If I had more time, we could send a letter to our banker in Boston and ask that the money be sent by special courier." She turned an anxious face toward Derrick. "Do you think we can convince these men to wait two or three more weeks?"

Derrick didn't think the men would wait at all. They had too much to lose if they were caught, and every delay increased that chance. "They might think it's a trap," he said cautiously, then saw her stricken face. "But don't worry. I will not allow anything to happen to Royce."

And he wouldn't. Even if it meant giving up the *Sea Princess*. There would be other ships, Derrick decided. A whole fleet. All he had to do was work hard and be patient.

"If Royce is not fine . . ." She closed her eyes a second, then opened them. "If Royce is not fine, I will be alone. Derrick, he's all I have." Her voice quavered and Derrick put an arm about her shoulders and gave her a hug.

"No, he's not all you have. No matter what, you have me. And I will gladly give you the use of my mother." He smiled at her, thinking of how much his mother would love having a daughter to dote on.

Catherine stopped walking and looked up at him. "Thank you."

"You're welcome. Just don't be surprised if my mother decides you need fattening up. She thinks that about everyone who weighs less than a horse."

That drew a small chuckle and Derrick drew a relieved breath. Whatever happened, he and Catherine needed to be alert and ready, which was impossible if their thoughts dwelt on Royce. They reached the Red Rooster with moments to spare. Derrick bent his fingers a little, feeling the solid weight of the small sack of shot he'd wrapped into his palm. If his plan failed, at least he'd have the satisfaction of knowing his punches would be a bit harder.

Catherine smoothed her skirts, then met Derrick's gaze with a smile that trembled ever so slightly. "It's time. Are you ready?"

No, he wasn't. He glanced back down the street. "Come on, Smythe," he muttered. What was taking the man so blasted long?

But they couldn't afford to be late—the kidnappers had made that clear in their letter. Controlling his impatience, Derrick opened the door and motioned Catherine in. The interior of the inn was dark, and gradually their eyes adjusted to the light. Only one man stood in the room.

Cadaverously thin, he leaned on a broom. His suspicious gaze traveled over the two of them, then trailed behind to find George. "Here, now! No animals!"

"He's not an animal," Derrick said quickly. "He's a . . . ah, a good luck charm."

"I don't care if he were a statue made o' gold. I don't allows animals in me inn."

Derrick ground his teeth, wondering if he could just flatten the cretin and get on with it. But Catherine moved ahead, saying crisply to the innkeeper, "If you want the dog removed, *you'll* have to send him away."

The man eyed George uneasily. "Does he bite?"

"Only rude people," Catherine replied.

Derrick choked.

The innkeeper gave a visible start, then held his broom directly in front of him. "Ye can't be serious!"

"Oh, but I am." Catherine pursed her lips. "I suppose you could chase the beast off with your broom. He doesn't *usually* bite people with brooms."

George panted happily, a large drip of white spittle on his lower lip.

"What do ye mean he don't *usually* bite people wif brooms?"

"Only that he hasn't bitten anyone with a broom *lately*."

"Oh. He . . . he *is* a big 'un," the man said. He shifted uneasily from one foot to the other, his gaze suddenly returning to Catherine and Derrick. "Here, now! What are ye two awantin' in here, anyways? We ain't open yet."

Derrick stepped forward. "We're here for . . ." He glanced at the torn note he'd received that morning. "Mr. Crawford."

"Ye aren't his partner, are ye? The one bringin' him the money he's been natterin' about, are ye? 'Cause if ye are, he owes me fer two weeks."

"We're not his partner in anything. We're to meet him here to discuss some business."

"Business, eh?" The man's nose almost quivered with curiosity, but Derrick offered no more. After a moment, the man said testily, "Oh, go and see him then. He's at the top o' the stairs. Tell him he'd better pay his due today or I'm calling the constable, business partner or no, and he and those friends o' his can pay me from behind bars."

Derrick paused. "How many friends does Mr. Crawford have?"

"Two. A woman he calls 'wife,' though I think 'floozy' is more like it. And another man, who has been here but once or twice, and then only late at night."

"Only two?" Derrick asked quietly, hope rising.

"Well, three if ye count the sick one, and that's far too many fer jus' one room."

"Sick?" Catherine's voice quavered. "A large young man with blondish hair?"

"That'd be him. He's got the ague or something. All he does is sleep and eat, whenever Crawford bothers to roust him."

"He must be drugged," Derrick murmured. "But at least he's alive."

Catherine nodded, her face pale. "Come," she said, grabbing Derrick's arm and leading him toward the steps. "We must hurry." George followed along, wagging his tail.

Just as they reached the bottom step, the door burst open behind them and Smythe stood in the doorway. He was panting heavily, his red face damp from his exertions, a small pouch in his hand. "There ye are, Cap'n. Lord help us but Jenkins had to count out every blasted coin. I thought 'twould take a week."

Derrick strode across the room and took the pouch. He opened the top and peered in, satisfied at the yellow gleam he saw. "Very good."

"Aye, Cap'n. I wish ye'd let me help. I'm right good with a blunderbuss and—"

"No. We can't chance it."

"But Cap'n, if ye'd just see yer way to lettin' me and the men—"

"Return to the ship. That's an order."

The first mate's shoulders sagged. "Aye, Cap'n. As ye wish."

Derrick nodded, then stepped back. "We'll be back on ship within the hour."

"Aye." The first mate left, dragging his feet.

The innkeeper eyed them suspiciously. "Tell Crawford I don't want no more of him if there's going to be such strange happenings."

Derrick took Catherine by the elbow and led her up the stairs. Halfway up, he stopped and handed the bag to Catherine.

"What's this?" she asked.

"Gold. Enough to buy Royce's freedom."

"Derrick!" She threw her arms about his neck.

He held still, savoring the feel of her, but making no move to prolong the contact. "It won't do us any good here on the steps. Let's get it to those bastards who took your brother."

She released him, her face shining with happiness. "I don't know how to thank you. Where did you get it?"

"I'll tell you when this is over."

She nodded, holding the gold with both hands as if afraid to lose it. Derrick led the way to the top of the steps, George shuffling behind. Every once in a while, the dog would stop to sniff, and a wet spot appeared on the steps.

When they reached the first door, Derrick rapped sharply on it.

It opened the second his knuckles hit the wood. A short, fat man stood in the opening, his thinning hair slicked to one side, a large purple birthmark adorning his forehead.

"Crawford?" Derrick asked.

"That's me." The man's little eyes darted from Derrick to Catherine, then back. "Who're ye?"

"Catherine Markham," Derrick said.

"And that?" Crawford eyed George with an uncertain gaze.

"Miss Catherine's dog. She never goes anywhere without him."

"I see. Do ye haf the money?"

Catherine held out the pouch.

The man's eyes widened. "Ye *do* haf the money! Well, that's—" He stopped and licked his lips, his gaze fixed greedily on the bag, a crafty expression in his eyes. "I suppose ye might as well come in." He glanced at the dog. "Exceptin' the mutt."

"Oh, please let us bring him," Catherine said. "He's very well behaved."

Derrick almost choked at that. The man didn't look too convinced either. "I don't know," he said, eyeing George warily.

"Please?" Catherine said softly. "He's a very friendly puppy." As if to prove her point, she patted the dog, who immediately sank into a pile of lumpy fur at her feet, panting as if exhausted from climbing the stairs.

Derrick eyed the man curiously. He'd been expecting the hardest, most flintlike villain to be holding Royce— someone like DeGardineau or one of his men. Instead, Crawford seemed . . . harmless. Everything about him was soft, unformed, uncertain.

Crawford hitched up his pants. "Don't want that mutt in here. Can he sit outside?"

"No!" Catherine said. She looked piteously at the man, tears welling in her eyes. "He's all I've got left in the whole world. Ever since my brother disappeared, George has been my constant companion and—"

"There, now!" The fat man eyed Catherine nervously.

"There's no sense in bawlin'! Ye can have yer mutt if ye'll keep him quiet."

Catherine's smile burst forth once more. "Thank you, sir!"

To Derrick's surprise, Crawford blushed, a faint smile creasing his plump face. "Well, now, there's no need to get all blustery on me. I ain't an evil man, which I do hopes ye remember when ye've got yer brother back home wif ye."

"Crawford," said a sharp feminine voice from inside the room. "Bring them in and stop gabbin'."

The fat man's reddened cheeks got darker. "Yes, yes. Sorry, Lila, m'dear. But I've good news; they haf the money."

"Do they?" she said. "Haf ye seen it?"

He gave a nervous laugh and stepped back from the doorway. "Come in, come in! We need to hurry, we do."

Derrick straightened his shoulders and followed Catherine through the door. *Please let everything go well,* he prayed. *Just this once. For Catherine.*

Crawford glanced down the hallway as if to make certain no one else was with them before he followed them into the room. It was surprisingly spacious, with a large rickety bed in one corner, a table and some broken chairs in front of an empty fireplace. A slovenly dressed female sat in one of the chairs, her mussed red dress and faded brown hair a fitting decoration for her harsh face.

But it was the pistol that lay on the table before her

that drew Derrick's attention. He raised his hands. "We aren't armed."

"Ye'd better not be." Lila sneered. "Or Markham gets it between the eyes." She nodded toward the bed and it took Derrick a moment to see who she was talking about.

On the far side of the bed, barely visible from where they stood, was Royce. He lay without moving, his face pale and streaked with dirt. "Royce!" Catherine flew to his side, George lumbering behind her.

Derrick had Crawford by the throat and slammed against the wall before the man could so much as swallow. "If my friend is unable to stand and walk from this room by himself, I will take the cost from your hide. One bloody inch at a time."

Crawford's mouth opened and shut, and his eyes were so wide they appeared ready to pop from his head. A thin bit of spittle gathered at the corners of his mouth.

"Easy now," Lila said. "I don't mind ye smackin' him around a bit, but if ye don't let him breathe, he'll wet hisself and then where will ye be?"

"How's Royce?" Derrick asked Catherine.

"He's alive," she replied. "I need some water."

Derrick slowly released Crawford, who staggered to a small table. "Here's ye go!" He picked up a glass and carried it back to Catherine, his face still red. "I tried to take care o' him the best I could—"

"Ye babied him, ye have," Lila said, her thick lip curled. "Even tucked the bloke in wif a blanket each and every night."

Catherine didn't comment. She was too busy talking to Royce, her voice thick with emotion. "What is making him sleep like that? Laudanum?" Derrick asked.

Crawford nodded. "Just a wee dram each night and then again in the mornin'."

Lila sniffed. "Enough talkin'. Where's the money?" She rubbed her nose with the back of her hand. "'Tis lucky you came when you did. We're tired of tendin' the fool. I ain't a nursemaid, ye know."

Derrick had a pretty good idea what Lila was, but he held his peace. Instead he flashed a glance at Catherine, who was holding a glass to Royce's mouth. "Can he walk?"

"I don't know," Catherine said, her eyes bright with tears. She shot a hard look at Crawford. "He's so thin. Didn't you feed him?"

Crawford held out his hands. "Here, now! I did the best I could. That sorry bloke only gave me enough money to live off of fer two weeks and I didn't—"

"Bloke? What bloke?" Derrick asked, his brows lowered.

Crawford bit his lip, while Lila gave a snort of disgust. "Go ahead and tell 'em everything, will ye?" she said sarcastically.

The pudgy man shook his head. "Sorry about that.

Let's just say that Lila and I did what we could."

Catherine helped her brother to his feet. Royce was as tall as Derrick, but he had Catherine's fair coloring. She'd used her skirt to wipe the dirt from his face, though Derrick could see that it was covered with a rough, golden beard.

"Derrick," he managed to rasp out, trying to smile through cracked and dry lips. "I knew you'd come."

"Derrick?" Catherine said. "What about me?"

Royce's smile broke forth like a sunset as he looked fondly at his sister. "I knew you'd come, too. But I didn't know that you'd be bringing *him*." He nodded toward George, who was loudly sniffing one corner of the room.

"He wouldn't let me leave him behind," Catherine said.

Crawford leaned toward Derrick and said in an almost kindly voice, "Some food and sleep and he'll be right as rain."

Derrick refused to believe Crawford had planned this kidnapping. But who? Derrick straightened. "We must be going."

"In a hurry to leave?" Lila sneered. She slouched in her chair, her dress twisted about her plump body, the neckline embarrassingly low. "Think ye're too fine fer us, don't ye?"

"There now, Lila," Crawford said, an embarrassed smile on his face. "Let the gentleman alone."

"I ain't leavin' no one alone until we gets our money."

She leaned forward, her hard eyes on Derrick.

Catherine handed over the small sack of gold. Within seconds, Lila had poured it onto the table and was stacking the coins into piles. After a few moments, she grinned, showing two blackened teeth. "It's all here, Mick. All fifty coins."

Crawford rubbed his hands together. "There ye go, then! Ye can take yer brother, miss, and be gone."

Lila poured the coins back in the bag and tied the top.

Derrick glanced at Catherine. She slid one of Royce's arms about her neck while Derrick took the other and they helped him toward the door. George immediately followed.

They were out of the room in a flash, hurrying downstairs as quickly as they could. The scrawny innkeeper was nowhere to be seen as they assisted Royce through the taproom. Catherine tightened her hold on Royce. He was staggering, trying to hurry, but too weak to do more than drag his feet, one slow step at a time.

"Hold on," she commanded.

"I am holding on," he protested. He sent her a curious glance. "Just when did you get so bossy? I'm surprised Derrick let you on his ship."

She'd thought she'd never hear her brother's teasing voice again. Unexpected tears sprang to her eyes. "Save your strength. You can torment me all you want after you are well."

He flashed a weak grin and they made their way to the door.

Just as they reached it, it flew open. A jaunty figure stood in the doorway, blocking their way. Catherine gasped as she recognized the man. It was DeGardineau. And in his hand was a gleaming pistol.

CHAPTER SIXTEEN

"What do you want?" Catherine bit out. "We have no more gold."

DeGardineau advanced into the room, the pistol pointed directly at her. Catherine started to protest, but Royce squeezed her shoulder in warning.

The pirate's teeth flashed. "Well, well. Isn't this a cozy little group?"

Catherine shivered at his cold voice. George, feeling the tension in her, leaned against her legs and looked up at her with a questioning gaze.

Upstairs, the sound of a door being thrown open echoed loudly, followed by hurried footsteps. Seconds later, Crawford thumped down, Lila behind him. The two were dressed for travel and carried a number of scuffed bags. They came to an abrupt halt when they caught sight of DeGardineau.

Crawford swallowed noisily. "M-Mr. DeGardineau. When did ye—I didn't know ye were coming."

The Frenchman looked less than pleased. "Obviously. Are you going somewhere?"

"Ah, no! No, of course not," the man replied, looking

wildly at the door as if considering a mad dash for freedom.

"Excellent," DeGardineau said. "Because I'd hate to think that you were attempting to cheat me."

Crawford's face burned a bright red. "I would never do such a thing!"

Lila nodded. "Lud, no! W-we were just taking some old things out to ah, to sell them. Old clothes and the like."

DeGardineau regarded them with a sneer. "Do not try my patience more than you already have! You were told to send these two away the second they showed up. And on no account were you to let Royce Markham out of your sight. It's a good thing that I arrived when I did."

"Wait a minute," Catherine said, the truth dawning on her. "*You* arranged the kidnapping."

The Frenchman bowed. "None other."

"But I thought Uncle Elliot—" Catherine clamped her mouth closed.

"Your uncle is by no means innocent."

"He hasn't done as much as you. You, sir, are despicable."

"At times. But not as despicable as *Monsieur* Crawford and his ladybird, who cannot even follow a simple order. Then, to make matters worse, they try to cheat me."

"I'd never do such a thing!" Lila said in a shrill voice, "I didn't have nothin' to do with any o' this. It was all

Crawford's idea. He made me—"

"Shut up, you silly cow," the pirate said, sending her an exasperated look.

She turned a bright red, but said no more.

"As for you," DeGardineau snarled at Crawford, "explain how you came to allow our golden goose to escape."

"Ye said they wouldn't have the money and we were to send them on their way after makin' sure they seen that Mr. Markham was breathin'. But they *did* have the gold, so I—"

"They had gold?" DeGardineau sent a sharp look at Derrick. "Where did you get it?"

Derrick didn't answer and Catherine frowned. Where *had* he gotten the gold?

"Ah," DeGardineau said, his brows raising. "You put the *Sea Princess* against a note, didn't you? A risky move, my lad. And very, very foolish."

Catherine couldn't believe her ears. "Derrick? Did you do that? Did you risk your ship?"

"It wasn't a risk. I'll pay it off once I make this next shipment."

"You shouldn't have taken such a chance," Royce ground out. He swayed a little on his feet, though he managed a warm smile. "But thank you."

Derrick shrugged. "It was the least I could do. You trusted me when no one else would."

"Such devotion." DeGardineau flicked a cold glance at Crawford. "Hand it over."

"O' course!" The man began fumbling in his pockets. "Here's the gold. I was goin' to bring it to ye as soon as—"

"Spare me your lies," DeGardineau said, slipping the bag of gold into his own pocket. He gestured to the stairs. "Why don't you and the lovely Lila return to your lodgings while I handle this situation? I will deal with the two of you in a moment."

Crawford hurriedly gathered his bags. "Come along, Lila! We'll wait upstairs fer Mr. DeGardineau to finish his business." He sent Derrick an apologetic glance, but he was obviously too frightened to think of helping.

Lila gathered her bags, though she grumbled loudly about being bossed about. Crawford didn't give her time to say much, for he grasped her arm and tugged her out of sight up the stairs.

Catherine took a slow breath, tightening her hold on Royce. She could feel the thunderous beat of his pulse and she realized that he was weaker than she'd realized. He was fighting just to stay upright and he wouldn't be able to make a mad dash to safety. Not until the sedative he'd been given had a bit more time to wear off.

She glanced at Derrick. He returned her look with a somber one of his own and she realized that he had reached the same conclusion. They needed time.

"DeGardineau," Catherine said, "I don't understand

about the kidnapping. What did my uncle have to do with this?"

The pirate pursed his lips. His glance slid past Catherine to the open door that led out into the alleyway. "Perhaps you should ask him that question yourself."

Catherine turned. There, standing in the doorway, was Uncle Elliot. Neatly dressed as always, his white hair was carefully combed, his boots shined to perfection. He looked respectable and forthright, but there was a hard look on his face that Catherine had never seen. "Uncle Elliot?"

DeGardineau's smile widened. "Tell them, *Monsieur* Markham. Tell them your part in this."

Elliot came farther into the room. He frowned at the pirate. "What are you doing here?"

"I could ask you the same question," DeGardineau retorted.

"I was sent a note." Elliot pulled a torn and dirty piece of paper from his pocket. "It seems to have been written by the same——"

"Those traitors!" DeGardineau whipped a hard glance at the stairway where Crawford and Lila had disappeared. "They were trying to collect as much money as they could. I will not tolerate such insubordination!"

Elliot frowned. "What do you mean? What traitors? How could——" Comprehension dawned. He shook his head as if to clear it. "*You* were the one who had Royce kidnapped? But why—how— I don't understand."

Derrick smiled grimly. "I think I do. DeGardineau saw the opportunity to make money and a lot of it. He sent you the ransom note knowing full well that you wouldn't want Royce to return. Then he came to you and offered to make certain that it never happened."

"I—I never asked him to harm anyone. I just wanted proof that Royce was—" Elliot caught his nephew's gaze and he flushed. "I truly believed you were already dead, Royce. I just needed evidence so that the estate could be settled quickly."

"Why would that matter to you unless . . ." Royce's frown deepened. "You were going to claim it all for yourself."

"I just wanted my due! I never wanted anyone to get hurt."

"Didn't you?" Derrick asked. "What about the attack on the *Sea Princess*? You told DeGardineau that Catherine was on my ship. You asked him to attack it. When that failed, you sent him to steal the gold and do away with us."

"You don't understand! It was all his idea! I just wanted—" He caught himself, sending a hard stare at the pirate. "You played me for a fool! And now all is lost."

DeGardineau curled his lip. "Do not be such a weakling! If you wish, you can still rescue this situation. We could kill them. I owe St. John a bullet. As for your niece and nephew, they stand between you and what you want."

A look of horror passed over Elliot's face. "I—I can't just—"

"Yes, you can," DeGardineau said. "Do you want the money and your precious house?"

"Yes, but—"

"Then do what you must! Take out your gun."

Slowly, Elliot reached into his pocket and withdrew a silver-handled pistol.

"Shoot the girl first," DeGardineau said, after sending a thoughtful stare at Royce, who was leaning heavily against the back of a chair. "I will shoot St. John."

A cold trickle of fear raced through Derrick. He'd engaged in dozens of bloody battles from the decks of ships, faced down ferocious cannon fire that had reduced other men to tears, and fought the fury of a hundred storms, all without a flicker of trepidation. But the sight of Elliot's trembling gun pointing toward Catherine sent a tremor of pure fear through him. Death to him was nothing. Seeing Catherine harmed was everything. He would not allow it to happen. "Elliot."

The older man reluctantly pulled his gaze from Catherine.

"Do you trust DeGardineau? Once you have killed us, he will hold that over you for the rest of your life. You will never have peace. He will make you pay and pay and pay."

Derrick could see the indecision in the man's face.

"Do not listen to them," DeGardineau snapped. "They

will say anything to save themselves."

Elliot wiped his forehead with his sleeve and Derrick could see how much his hands trembled. He was torn, uncertain, and afraid.

Elliot looked at DeGardineau and blinked. Once. Twice. "He's right," he said slowly. "If I do this, nothing will stop you from stealing everything I thought to gain." He lowered his gun. "I can't. DeGardineau, it stops here."

"It stops when I say it stops," the pirate snapped. It happened so quickly that no one saw it coming. One second the pirate was standing facing them, his face dark and bitter. The next he'd lifted his pistol and fired. Elliot staggered back and George bounded to his feet.

DeGardineau turned the pistol toward Catherine. "No one moves, or the girl dies."

Elliot stared dully down at the blood spreading over his coat. "You shot me."

"*Oui.* I have no need of a man with a conscience." The Frenchman pointed the gun at Catherine's head. "Now for you."

George's ears perked forward and he growled.

DeGardineau squinted down the barrel of his pistol.

"*No,*" Elliot cried, though it was a whisper more than anything else. He tried to lift his gun, but he didn't have the strength. Tears filled his eyes. "Catherine. I'm sorry. So . . . sorry." He sank to the floor in a heap.

DeGardineau cocked his pistol.

Derrick tensed, ready to leap in front of Catherine. *God help us all.*

A low, deep sound rumbled beside Derrick and he glanced down at George. The dog stood, fur bristled, his lips curled as he growled, his eyes never leaving DeGardineau.

"*Mademoiselle,*" the pirate said, a gleam in his eye. "Say good-bye."

"George," Derrick snapped. "*At him!*"

George leaped, all one hundred and twenty pounds of furry dog slamming into the pirate. DeGardineau didn't have time to do more than grunt before he was knocked to the ground. His gun flew from his hand as the dog's huge paws slammed into his chest.

The two rolled in a jumble of fur and clothing as George bit whatever appendage he could find. The dog's growls and the pirate's frantic cries filled the air as they rolled. Derrick scrambled to collect both DeGardineau's and Elliot's guns. He pressed one into Catherine's hand and kept the other.

The growls and cries had stopped. George held his prisoner captive with his huge jaws around the man's neck. Every time DeGardineau attempted to move, George would tighten his jaw until the pirate stopped squirming.

"St. John," DeGardineau gasped. "Make . . . him . . . stop." The pirate had lost his gun, his clothing was ripped and torn, and he had a deep gash down one side of his face. He was terrified, and George had such a tight grip on the man's neck that he could barely breathe.

"Cap'n!" Smythe and Bransom stood in the doorway, several other crew members peering over their shoulders.

The first mate looked at where Elliot lay on the floor in a pool of blood. "Cap'n, I know ye told us not to come, but—"

"I'm glad you're here," Derrick said. He leaned over DeGardineau. "If I get the dog off of you, will you tell the truth about my father?"

DeGardineau tried to nod, but couldn't. Finally, he gasped out a breathy, "Yes!"

"Very well. But I warn you—if you do not, I will bring the dog to visit you in prison. And I will not call him off again." Derrick stood. "George, release him."

The dog growled, but didn't move.

Derrick grabbed the dog by the ears. "Let go, George."

DeGardineau moaned, closing his eyes. His face was turning slightly blue.

Derrick sighed. "Catherine?"

She looked up from where she'd been helping Royce into a chair, put the gun she'd been holding on a nearby table, and clapped her hands. "George, come!"

The dog sighed, then lifted his head, releasing the pirate, who slumped to the floor. With one last disdainful sniff, the dog ambled over to Catherine. She sank to her knees and put her arms about him, pressing her cheek against his neck.

Derrick, meanwhile, shoved the dazed DeGardineau into Smythe's arms. "Take him to the local authorities."

Smythe passed the man to Bransom. "You and Jacobs can see to that. And don't let him escape."

"Aye, aye!" They each took one of DeGardineau's arms and dragged him away.

Catherine tightened her grip on George's neck. She was vaguely aware of Derrick placing a blanket over Uncle Elliot and ordering someone to care for the body. Then he sent some men upstairs to take Crawford and Lila to the constable's office. Lila screamed that she was being abducted when the men dragged her down the steps and outside.

Moments later, the tavern was once again peaceful. Catherine raised her head just as Little helped Royce to the door. They paused there.

"Are you coming?" Royce asked, giving her a wan smile.

"In a moment," she said, her own knees shaking. "Are you feeling better?"

Little snorted. "He'll be as right as rain, as soon as I give him some of me special tonic."

Derrick came forward. "I'm certain Royce will enjoy it. Catherine and I will be with you in a moment."

"Aye, aye, Cap'n. We'll be right outside, when ye're ready."

Little and Royce walked outside and Catherine realized that only she and Derrick remained in the tavern. Her mind raced with the events of the past few hours—the delight of finding Royce still alive, the fear of being killed by DeGardineau and then Elliot, and last, her uncle's horrible death. A shiver racked her and she forced herself to her feet. At least her brother was safe and sound. The thought soothed her.

She dusted off her skirts and gave George a final pat. For some reason, she was embarrassed to look at Derrick. She owed him so much. But it was more than that. Simple gratitude had long ago changed into something more.

She loved him. The truth stole her breath. She loved him so much that it hurt to think of being without him. But did he love her? Could he ever feel the same way?

She had to know. And now, before they went back to the ship and she once again became just Royce's little sister. Catherine took a deep breath and slowly turned to face Derrick. He stood with his arms crossed, his feet planted as if he stood on the deck of the *Sea Princess*. His dark hair was mussed and she had to fight the urge to thread her fingers through it and straighten it.

Catherine cleared her throat. "We need to talk."

He lifted a brow. "Now? Once we get on board ship—"

"Once we get on board ship, we'll never have another minute alone. Derrick, I have to know something before . . ." The words tangled in her throat.

"Before what?"

She clasped her hands before her. Could he care for

her? Was it possible? His actions certainly made her think so. He was kind, gentle, and tender. But it was as if some barrier held him away. She took an unsteady breath and plunged forward. "Derrick, I think I . . ." What was she doing? She didn't think anything. She knew. She wiped her hands on her skirts and began again. "I love you."

His expression darkened. "You can't."

That astounded her. "Why not?"

"You have been raised to be the lady of a manor house, like High Hall. I'm a sea captain. I can't give you a tenth of what you have now. Not yet, anyway." He raked a hand through his hair, his expression tortured. "And even if I could . . ." He stopped and looked at her, his heart in his eyes. "Catherine, do you remember what DeGardineau said when he stole your gold?"

She thought a moment, struggling to remember. Suddenly, it came to her. "He said that you had no honor. That you were like him."

"It's true. I was a pirate. I captained a ship that sunk seven other ships. I was young and foolish, and excitement was all I cared about. At least so I thought, until my father was branded a traitor. Catherine, people believed what they did about my father all the more quickly because of who and what I was. That's why I have been searching for DeGardineau. To clear my father's name."

"And now you have," she said softly.

Derrick clenched his hands at his sides. It was all he

could do not to reach out and grab her and demand that she forgive him. But it wouldn't be right—Catherine deserved better than him.

He knew what would happen now. She would turn from him and never again look at him with that warm smile in her eyes. It was the thing he'd dreaded since the day she stepped on board his ship. He braced himself for her next words.

"This is difficult, isn't it?" She looked down at her feet, her lashes covering her expression. "Would you undo it if you could?"

"I would give my life to change it."

She nodded slowly and closed the space between them. When she reached his side, she placed a hand on his cheek, looking straight into his eyes. "I don't know who and what you were before we met. But I do know this; you have been nothing but gentle and kind and honest and generous since I asked you to help me rescue Royce. That is the man I fell in love with."

Derrick's heart thudded an extra beat. "Love? Even now that you know?"

She nodded, looking up at him with a clear gaze, her green eyes warm. And hidden in their depths was the smile he so loved. "Even if you don't love me in return, I will always love you, Derrick. Forever."

"You don't understand what I was. Catherine, I was a pirate, like DeGar—"

She placed her fingers over his lips. "Derrick, listen to me. I knew about your past before I sought you out at the Harbor. It doesn't matter what you were, it only matters what you are right now, at this moment."

Relief rushed through him and he captured her hand and held it. His feelings threatened to overwhelm him. Even knowing his worst flaws, she still cared for him. "I love you, Catherine. More than you will ever know." He pulled her closer and kissed her gently.

A huge, fluffy head pushed its way between them. Catherine stepped back, laughing, as George made his presence known. "I think he wants some attention."

Derrick scratched the dog's ears. "After what he did today, I'm going to see to it that he gets a tummy rub every day for the rest of his life."

Happy, George melted into a furry puddle on the floor. Derrick reached over and pulled Catherine to him once again. "Where were we?"

She lifted her face to his. His lips had just touched hers when—

"Hey," Royce said loudly from the doorway. "Are you two through talking yet? I'm hungry."

Derrick reluctantly broke away, though he kept his hands on Catherine's waist.

"Come on, Derrick," Royce called as he left. "You can 'talk' to Catherine once we get on ship."

Derrick sighed and his eyes met Catherine's. "You

know, I *was* going to warn him about Little's tonic, but I'll be damned if I'll say anything now."

She smiled and gave Derrick another kiss. He kissed her back, lifting her off her feet in the process. Afterward, he set her down and then leaned forward to whisper in her ear, "I love you, Catherine Markham. With all my heart."

DEAR READER:

Catherine is one brave girl—and lucky, too! Not only does she find Derrick in port, she cons him into taking her along in going after her brother. Not to mention that he falls in love with her along the way . . .

It's Derrick's pirate past that nearly keeps him apart from Catherine, but in the next Avon True Romance, it's Miranda and Shadow Walker's present that causes trouble for them. They're both very strong-minded and from two very different cultures—she's a US Cavalry major's daughter, he's a young Cheyenne warrior. The fact that Shadow Walker nabbed Miranda off her horse and is holding her as, well, a prisoner doesn't help matters much, either. But as MIRANDA AND THE WARRIOR will show you, there is a fine line between love and hate, as evidenced by the following excerpt.

Abby McAden
Editor, Avon True Romance

꧁

FROM
MIRANDA AND THE WARRIOR
by Elaine Barbieri

The morning dew left a silver sheen on the grass through which Miranda walked as she made her way to the spring. Glancing back, she saw the dark green trail her footsteps had left behind, the only marks to mar the beauty of the meadow that stretched out on all sides of her. She looked up at the snow-topped mountains in the distance that days of journeying had never seemed to bring any closer, and watched as the glow of the new day's sun rose up the slopes with breathtaking beauty.

A cool morning breeze caressed her skin and Miranda smiled. Shadow Walker had brought her to this spot two days earlier, explaining to her that it was a magical place where game was abundant and the days passed untouched, unaltered by the conflicts of the present.

Since they'd arrived, an easy pattern had been established between Shadow Walker and her. Shadow Walker had spent the mornings hunting while she worked around the camp, and during long afternoons they had eaten, swum, talked, and laughed. As evening shadows lengthened, their confidences had deepened, with Shadow Walker speaking of his youth with both sadness and joy, and of his hopes for times to come.

Miranda had not been so candid. Discomfort nudged at the knowledge that while she had spoken at length about her earlier life, she had avoided any references to her father's military status and rank, and the fact that he had often led his command against the Cheyenne. She had told herself that the intimacy of those moments was precious and too tenuous to risk—that she needed more time—but the passing hours only increased her difficulty.

Making her way toward the pool that glistened in the rising sun, Miranda glanced only briefly toward the knoll where her mount grazed protected from clear view. She knew that leaving the animal behind while he hunted was another sign of Shadow Walker's trust, and her discomfort deepened.

Miranda paused at the pool's edge, a recurring guilt plaguing her. What was her father doing now? Was he suffering because of her? She wished she could talk to him so she could apologize for her stubbornness in leaving the fort that day and tell him she loved him. She also wanted to tell him she had learned a lot since the day of her capture—about the Cheyenne way of life, the honor they accorded a battle that was well and honestly waged, and the value they placed on a person's given word. Most especially, however, she wanted to tell her father she knew now that Shadow Walker wasn't the savage everyone believed him to be, that he was just a man like any other.

Shadow Walker's image flashed before Miranda, and her heart skipped a beat. No, that was untrue. Shadow Walker was unlike any man she'd ever known.

A frown grew on Miranda's face as another thought nagged. But she couldn't tell her father all those things, because despite the beauty of the past few days, she was still a captive. Shadow Walker and she would eventually return to the Cheyenne camp, and when they did—she could not be certain how it would all end.

Suddenly unwilling to follow those thoughts any further, Miranda walked into the pond. The morning sun was bright on her head as the water soaked through her shirt to cool her skin. Closing her eyes, she forced away her concerns and floated motionlessly on the placid surface.

So absorbed was she that she did not hear the footsteps at the water's edge.

Shadow Walker swam underwater with long, powerful strokes. So relaxed was Miranda while floating on the surface of the pond that she had not heard him return from the hunt. Nor had she seen him turn his mount loose in the knoll before stripping down to his breechcloth to enter the water.

Reaching her side, Shadow Walker broke suddenly through the surface to Miranda's startled gasp. Momentarily silent, he stared into Miranda's face. Her great, clear eyes were wide with surprise. Heavy droplets of water clung to dark lashes that emphasized their startlingly light color. As he watched, the sun-kissed color of her fair cheeks flushed a darker shade that signaled pleasure at his return—pleasure that raised similar emotions in his own heart. A welcoming smile broke across her lips and he remembered a time when he had wondered with a sinking heart if that smile would ever shine for him.

Breaking the silence between them, Miranda said, "You surprised me. I didn't hear you come back."

Shadow Walker's smile dimmed at Miranda's comment. He replied, "In that lies the danger."

"Danger?" Miranda frowned and glanced around them. "What danger could threaten us in this beautiful place?"

Innocence.

Smiling again, Shadow Walker returned, "There is no danger while I am at your side, Miranda."

Emerging from the pond refreshed a short time later, Shadow Walker sat in the brilliant sunshine at the pool's edge. He smiled as Miranda sat down beside him. He watched as she wrung out her unbound hair, unconsciously separating the strands with her fingers as she said abruptly, "What did you mean when you said there was danger here?"

Shadow Walker did not respond.

"You didn't mean from animals, did you?"

"No."

"Tell me."

Shadow Walker responded evasively, "Caution is prudent wherever we are."

Miranda was confused. She had noted his concern when she failed to hear his return, but she sensed a deeper anxiety than the one he had voiced. She wanted to know what worried him.

But Shadow Walker resisted, and she pressed again, "Shadow Walker—"

"This place deceives, Miranda. Its beauty lulls the senses into believing that beyond this cool pond and green meadow where the sun shines and the sky is clear, blood is no longer spilled."

"But it's different here."

"Yes, here, close to sacred ground, the beauty remains, but it is fragile and must not be taken for granted."

"We're safe here, aren't we?"

Frowning, Shadow Walker replied, "I wish to speak of this no more, for to do so would be to compromise the short time here that remains."

The short time that remains.

"But you said—"

"I said that in this place there is peace. But it is unsafe to assume that we cannot be touched by the outside world here."

As if confirming Shadow Walker's words, the rumble of approaching hooves sounded in the distance. Miranda turned toward the sound with surprise. She squinted to identify the approaching figures, then gasped with incredulity as an army patrol rode into view.

The sight of the familiar blue uniforms raised Miranda's arm toward them in an exultant rush. Stunned when Shadow Walker snatched her down to the ground with his hand covering her mouth, then held her motionless with the weight of his body, she heard him whisper fiercely, "Hear what I say, Miranda, for I tell you now—there is only one way the soldiers will take you from me."

Shadow Walker's words froze Miranda's mind. Somehow unable to think past the inconceivability of the moment, she watched as the patrol drew nearer, then passed so close that she could see Lieutenant Hill's rigid expression, Will Blake's boyish frown, and Sergeant Wallace's invariable scowl. The hilts of their Army sabers glinted in the brilliant sun. Their sheathed rifles bounced against their mounts' sides—and Miranda closed her eyes.

The hoofbeats faded into the distance and Miranda opened her eyes again to see that the patrol had faded from view as well.

Releasing her abruptly, Shadow Walker stood up. His expression unreadable, he towered over her for long, silent moments before he said, "Ready yourself. It is time to leave."